WHEN STARS BURN OUT

CARRIE AARONS

Do you want your **FREE** Carrie Aarons eBook?

All you have to do is <u>**sign up for my newsletter**</u>, and you'll immediately receive your free book!

PROLOGUE
DEMI

Nine Years Ago

Glancing at the clock, I read the numbers one oh two. Nothing good happens at this time of night. At this hour, people should be sleeping. Or getting off a shift at the hospital. Or waking for a glass of water or to soothe a crying baby.

What they shouldn't be doing is sitting in front of a makeup mirror, the light all too bright contrasted in the darkness of the dorm room.

I slick on a coat of my favorite lipstick, careful to check that each eyelash is perfectly separated and inked with black mascara. Reaching for the hairbrush, I smooth out the curls I just spun into my hair, conscious of making it look effortless yet sexy.

I lie to myself, tell my stupid heart that this time he will notice the effort I put in. That when he opens his door, he'll finally realize that I'm beautiful and worth talking to, not just calling in the middle of the night for a fuck. Denial runs deep in my pores, and I pick out of the perfect "I just happened to be up and get out of bed to come over and hang out," outfit.

But, of course he won't recognize any of this. He will cover his mouth with mine, throw his hands in my hair, pull at my clothes ... and then I'll be a goner. All of the resolves I've built up, the hours I've spent talking to myself about how to form a real connection this time will go out the window.

And then I sit and wait, my foot nervously tapping as I stare at my phone waiting for the green light. Because when he calls, I come. I never have, and never will, say no.

My friends constantly look at me with disapproving stares when I make my way home with him from a party, or trek over to his dorm in the cold, or silently cry when as I watch him kiss other girls on campus.

I'm weak, and I know it. But, I'll never stop.

Because being with him is the best high I've ever known.

Because when he touches me, there is no better feeling in the entire world.

Because I'm the moth and he's the flame.

And the thing is, I know he wouldn't even notice if I burned completely.

1

DEMI

Watching someone else's dream come true is a blessing.

A tiny moment in which you have the privilege of witnessing that person's joy, their unadulterated happiness when the one thing they've wished for is standing right in front of them.

It's a high like no other, a selfish and selfless act at the same time. Knowing you are making it possible, and that you'd do whatever necessary to allow them to soar.

That's what I do for a living. I watch as children's greatest dreams are fulfilled, and then simultaneously as they themselves are pulled away from this world.

I watch them run with the greatest athletes on earth, scream their little lungs out on the rides at Disney, giggle as they make a cameo on their favorite television show. And then I swallow the bile in my throat as their mother's attach their oxygen tubes, or give them a needle in the middle of Magic Kingdom, or shield their brittle bodies from the sun because being outdoors too much will compromise their immune system.

Over the years, my stomach has become a vault of steel, I've trained my tear ducts to become immune. But there are still those cases that wiggle their way under your skin, flay you open and make you hurt.

That's how it is with Ryan Gunter. The seven-year-old boy who was recently diagnosed with the same cancer I watched dismantle my own brother years ago.

"We're taking this one." I throw the file on the gray-washed oak table in the conference room.

"Demi, we are so overloaded as it is, maybe we can wait until next month ..." My vice president of operations, Farrah, shifts her eyes to the six other employees sitting around the table.

"I don't care. We're taking this one. I'll work the extra hours, get the paperwork passed through, I just ... this is one of mine." My light brown bangs fall a little into my eyes, and I realize I need to visit my salon for a cut.

Every so often, one of my staff at Wish Upon a Star would claim a case as *theirs*. Some illness, or a kid they became attached to from reading the file, that was close to their heart. And even if we were buried in work, even if it would burden us to take on another case, no one said a thing.

That was how it was now, a silent compliance falling over the table.

"Okay, Gina, tell us where we are at with the other cases." My hands smooth down my hunter green dress, the fit and flare a good color match for my creamy complexion and milk chocolate-colored hair.

I was the boss, the face of my nonprofit. While it felt materialistic and superficial to worry about curling my hair and strapping on stilettos each morning, it also showed the world that I was a serious business woman. And that gained me clients who would work with us, so it was a necessary evil.

My marketing coordinator ran through the current children we were trying to grant wishes for, and what was left in each case to get it done. Currently, we had ten children who needed their wishes fulfilled in the next two months. My team was talking to the professional baseball team in New York, a connection at the White House, a resort in Aruba, and the pop princess who was on her million-dollar world tour right now.

I'd started my company five years ago on a wish and a prayer with the inheritance I'd received when my grandfather passed. He had always supported my dreams, and when he'd left this world, I knew that it was time to do what I'd been thinking about for years. Every time I'd settle into my six-hundred-square-foot apartment back then, after a long day at the public relations firm I did grunt work for, I would think about starting this nonprofit that made children with incurable illnesses happy. To give a little part of joy to the families who were suffering, because I knew all too well what that was like.

With hard work and elbow grease and just a few too many hours sucking up to useful connections, I'd built my business into a wonderful, successful charity. People heard the name Demi Rosen, and they knew I could get things handled. They knew I could make dreams come true.

"Let's get a drink, I think after today, we've earned it." Farrah comes into my office at the end of the day.

Looking around the room that is my private office, closed off from the rest of the beautiful space Wish Upon a Star occupies in one of the nicest buildings in downtown Charlotte, I think she's right. My office, as much of the entire space, is primarily made of floor-to-ceiling glass windows that overlook the bustling city. While it isn't New York or Chicago, our secondary city is a busy place in its own right. Modern furniture, desks with each employee's personal touch, and walls lined with black and white photos of our wishes granted over the years complete the space.

The one expense I do splurge on is fresh flowers weekly for

our office. It seems to keep everyone's spirits up, and when families come to visit, a beautiful bouquet just sets them at ease or gives them the smallest boost of cheer.

"I think I'll take you up on that." I pick up my leather satchel and follow her out.

We arrive at McDaniels, the bar around the corner, in the swing of happy hour, and are lucky to find a table.

"Why do I feel like we get older every time we come here?" Farrah's trim snakeskin patterned slacks and white bell sleeve blouse make her look anything but.

She's edgier than I am, with a jet-black bob and a nose ring. When I'd first interviewed her, I hadn't thought we would be able to work together. But, it turned out, Farrah was the yin to my yang when it came to running the business. And she has also slowly developed into one of my closest friends.

"Because most of these kids don't even know what the word 401(k) means yet." I flag down a bartender and order us two gin and tonics, having been very practiced at the two-for-one special they ran.

At thirty years old, Farrah and I were on the older end of the scene here, but it wasn't as if we looked the part.

Farrah stretches her neck. "Damn, I need to get laid."

She was, unlike me, very casual about sex. Often, she'd regale me with her tales of hookups gone wrong, and gone oh so right.

"Well, you have many eligible men to choose from." I waved my hand around the bar.

She shrugged. "Eh, these are boys. I'd eat them alive. But it doesn't mean they're not your speed. Let me be your wing woman."

She's pleaded this before. "Nope, you know my rule. No dates, no men."

"Are you a lesbian? Come on, seriously, you know you can tell me." Farrah has posed this question before.

I chuckle. "I would have no problem telling you if I was, but no. Honestly, it's just simpler this way, cleaner."

She sighs and turns away, people watching and finishing her drink.

I nod to myself, knowing I'm right. If you never let anyone in, at least intimately, you never got hurt.

And I was never going to allow myself to be hurt again.

There is something severely humbling about getting older.

Not just in the mental sense, the learning and wisdom that comes along with adding years to one's life.

No, for an athlete it is always about the physical. The aching bones that become harder to ignore each time you come off the field. The joints that crack with each movement when you get out of bed in the morning. The muscles that can no longer lift the amount of weight they used to.

And then eventually, the injury comes. It could be one, it could be many. But there is always that defining moment when you know your career has reached its peak, and now you're on the slope tumbling down to retirement.

At the ripe old age of thirty, a year after I'd torn my meniscus, I knew that I was already halfway down that hill.

I circle my hip, warming my right leg up in the training facility that looks nothing like the one I inhabited for the last ten years. Because what also comes along with getting older, at least as a professional football player, is getting traded. It's leaving the organization you've bled for, for years because they could sell you on the cheap to a team who could use a seasoned, even if he's not one hundred percent, veteran.

I'm bitter, yes, but that's the way of the league. Not that Charlotte isn't nice; it's warmer than Massachusetts. I attended college here, it's sort of like coming home. It has a nice downtown and a good fan base, the apartment I was set up with isn't half bad.

"How is the knee feeling?" Anthony, the trainer I've been working with since signing with the North Carolina Cheetahs, walks into the state of the art facility.

The best lifting equipment, lines of treadmills and bikes, weights, medicine balls, resistance bands ... all in the bright warehouse painted in the team colors of maroon and gold. It looks similar to every other professional athletic center I've ever been in. In fact, this is the room I've spent the most time in since moving back to Charlotte two months ago. That's kind of pathetic.

"Feeling loose, which is good. I think I'll be good to go for practice this week." We were a week out of the regular season, and I'd missed training camp.

After tearing the muscles in my knee halfway through last season, I'd elected to have the surgery and make the rough battle of a comeback. At thirty, many were counting me out. But I was going to prove those fucking talking heads wrong.

"Good, 'cause I'm going to push you to the limit today." He smiles like he'll enjoy my pain.

Which he probably will.

Anthony walks to the radio, tuning the Sirius to a heavy metal station that he knows will get my head in the right space.

"Hey, have you taken some time to learn the city yet?" He sits down next to the mat where I stretch out.

I repeat my physical therapy exercises, three reps before I

attempt to work out. "Honestly, I've just been trying to get as healthy as possible to play."

"I get that. But ... you should get out for a little. Walk around, see how the fan base and the people here operate. Sometimes, it will give you even more motivation. Remember, football is as much of a mental game as it is a physical one."

He was right, of course, but I hadn't allowed myself to have a social life in years. The occasional drink with a teammate, a dinner with my brother when he came to town, the rare date ... but that was about it. My life, for the last seven years, had been miserably lonely.

Anthony sees my hesitance. "Listen, I'll tell you what. I'll buy you a beer after I whoop your ass for the next hour."

Warring with myself, I decide I kind of need the relaxation. "Okay, you've got a deal."

Two hours later, the waitress sets our burgers down in front of us.

My mouth waters and I now believe Anthony when he tells me this tiny restaurant off Tryon Street has some of the best food in town. It's been so long since I lived here, I have no idea what restaurants are good anymore. Everything has changed in the eight years I've been gone, including me.

I wash down my first beer, a hoppy IPA, before digging in.

"Shit, I needed this after the hell you unleashed on me today."

He laughs. "For an old geezer in this league, you can surprisingly hold your own."

I give him a stink eye. "Asshole. I'll go toe to toe with any of these hot shots coming out of the draft."

"I don't doubt it. Honestly, I think you'll be ready to play. That's the recommendation I'm going to give Coach Bryant."

He shouldn't be telling me this, but I appreciate the openness. "Thanks, man. You don't have to compromise yourself for me, but I know your word will go a long way with Coach."

I hadn't spent much time with Jason Bryant, the head coach I was playing under now, but he seemed like a stand-up guy. And like Anthony, he'd shot straight with me in each interaction we'd had so far. There was something to be said for being an older player. Since the coaches and staff were closer to your age than the cocky boys coming up from college, there was some kind of unspoken respect.

I lived and breathed football, it was my life. But sometimes, I wanted to shut down shoptalk. And right now, was one of those times. "So, you've been with the organization how long?"

He puts down his napkin, covered in barbecue sauce from his burger, and clears his throat. "About six years, and it's a great place to be. The owners are great, coaches listen to us trainers, and they're a no-nonsense club, so they don't allow a lot of goons on the roster. My wife loves it here; our daughter just started kindergarten ... it's just a great city to live in."

"I didn't realize you were married."

Anthony pulls a necklace out from under his shirt, a wedding band hanging in the middle. "Ten years, dude. I keep my ring here, don't want the weights to scratch it. But, Lucy, that's my wife, she's the best thing that ever happened to me."

By the look in his eyes, I know he means it. I've seen two different emotions from people who are married; bliss or misery. Anthony is obviously in the former, and a little part of me burns with jealousy. I've never come close to that, but lord knows I spent years being too fucking selfish to even realize that I wanted something like what he had.

Something like what my parents had.

Anthony is talking, but the whooshing in my ears drowns him out. Sadness fills every pore, and even seven years later, it feels like someone has taken a stake to my heart each time I think about them.

Maybe I can finally find that. Maybe this move, although involuntary, will be good for me. Maybe Charlotte will bring a new beginning as my career hits its end.

3

DEMI

A week later, it's the day of our meeting with Ryan, his family, and the football player who will help fulfill his wish.

Having met with the family and this special little boy in the hospital earlier in the week, where I sat with them while Ryan received a chemotherapy treatment, I couldn't wait to introduce him. Couldn't wait to watch his face light up and hear all of the adorable questions he'd ask his hero.

He reminded me so much of Julian; the same diagnosis, almost the same age, that light brown hair that has started to fall out in clumps.

"Everything is in place?" I ask Gina.

With everything else we had going on, along with the two society events I'd attended this week in hopes of recruiting new board members, I hadn't had time to plan every nitty-gritty detail of Ryan's wish. I was more interested in getting to know the family, which I'd started to do with my visit to the hospital. But, I knew that his dream included the football team here in Charlotte, and something about sitting on the sidelines at a game. Gina and Farrah had overseen the actual acquiring and scheduling, and I'm sure we are going to meet with Harry, the public relations rep for the Cheetahs.

"We're all set, boss. He's already here, talking with Ryan and his family. Insisted on coming himself, instead of Harry. Although Harry does send his best." Gina points to our conference room, the glass-encased hub sitting in the middle of our office that you could look right into.

I turned, my dark chocolate eyes landing on the figure sitting next to the sweet little boy.

My hands began to shake. The back of my neck tingled with anticipation. My stomach became a knot of nerves, sending up an anxious noise that I had to swallow in my throat.

He wasn't even in the same room as I was, my position to him staring through the glass walls of the conference room, and yet he could still affect me like this.

I was shaking in my nicest Ann Taylor suit, all because Paxton Shaw was, once again, in the same building as I was.

Sandy blond hair cropped short, stunning green eyes, a black stud in his left ear, the strong as steel jaw that is now covered in a sandy blond beard. He's a man now, so different than the boy I once knew, but still so much the same.

My ovaries could barely contain themselves. I wanted to smack them, traitorous organs.

"Why is the most famous tight end in the league sitting in our conference room?" Gina walks up beside me, her eyes almost undressing him across our office.

"Tight end?" My tongue practically falls out of my mouth thinking about how firm his ass was when I used to see it.

"Seriously? With all of the football teams we're around while granting wishes and you still haven't picked up any terms or positions? Demi, I'm ashamed. That's Paxton Shaw, all-star tight end in the National Football League. He's got like, three Super Bowl rings, his name in record books, and is fine as hell to boot."

She'd mistaken me. Of course, I knew who Paxton Shaw was, and I knew he was a professional athlete, Facebook be damned. But, I knew who he was for a very different reason than the hundreds of thousands of Americans who worshipped at his feet every Sunday.

It had been eight years since I'd seen him, but it was as if I could feel Paxton's hands over every inch of my body.

My feet, somehow, miraculously move, following Gina. I have to attend this meeting, and I try to mask my emotions, lock them away. I hope I'm doing a good job, but hell if I can tell. Internally, every warning bell is going off.

I entered the room, feeling like all the air left as the glass door shut behind me.

Ryan, his parents, and Joe, our scheduling coordinator, looked up as Gina and I entered. Paxton's gray eyes turned a split-second later, taking us in.

And ... he completely doesn't recognize a thing about me.

I flush, I can't help it, embarrassment suffusing my bones. Oh my God, he has no idea who I am.

I've had vivid, sexual dreams about him for years. Have gone over and over in my head what I did wrong for him not to want me. Thought about how my life would be different if we had committed to each other.

And Paxton Shaw has absolutely no recollection of my face whatsoever.

"Hello, everyone. Ryan, it's so good to see you again. How you feeling, kiddo?" I snap into professional mode, not wanting to give that man anymore of my attention.

"Hi, Miss Demi! I got a signed jersey!" He holds up the shirt on the table in front of him, his crooked smile adorable with its missing teeth.

"That is so cool! I hope these adults aren't boring you too much." I wink conspiratorially at him.

He giggles, and I look to his mother, who has tears in her eyes. This is probably the best he's felt in a year, and I know what it's like to be grateful for that. I sit down, next to her, squeezing her hand.

Joe starts the meeting, detailing what game Ryan and his family will go to, how they'll take part in practice beforehand, his position standing with the coaches during the first and second quarter.

I know it's awkward that I haven't greeted Paxton yet, haven't extended my hand and thanked him for being here.

I turn to face him, painting a fake smile on my face. I can do this, I'm stronger than I once was.

This man, the one sitting directly across the table from me, had been my kryptonite. He'd strung me along, on and off, for two whole years.

And in the end, had ruined me for anyone else, forever.

Ten Years Ago

Ludacris bumps over the speakers, red cups littering every surface and a random smoke machine pouring out over the makeshift dance floor.

I'd given myself an irregular night out, my best friend and roommate, Chelsea, convincing me that I couldn't spend another Friday in our dorm room watching The West Wing on my DVD player.

Surprisingly, I was having a good time. That could be the four Jell-O shots swimming around in my stomach, but my body felt like it was floating, and I felt the rhythm of the music move me.

My eyes land across the dance floor, to where a group of people crowd around someone I can't quite make out. I dance closer, straying from my group of friends who dance in a semi-circle, some of them grinding on guys and some just doing their own thing.

As I make my way over, some of the people disperse, and he stands up from where he was lounging on one of the massive speakers blasting music through the house.

Well over a foot taller than I am, with unruly blond hair tucked behind his ears, dark denim covering his long legs, and a white V-neck

T-shirt barely containing the mass of muscles that constitute his arms. A diamond stud winks from one earlobe, and it's cheesy but also screams bad boy.

I've never gone for the bad boy.

And yet ... there is something about this guy that draws me toward him until I'm practically sitting in his lap. Maybe it's the drinks making me bold, or maybe it's the need to do something so out of character that my heart screams for it.

But I find myself initiating conversation with the hottest guy I've ever laid eyes on.

"Hey." *I put a little flirt into my game, planting a hand on my hip and leaning into him, surprising myself even if it was just one word.*

His eyes, bright green even in the dark light of the house party, scan me up and down. I feel naked, undressed for him. It's thrilling and dirty, and I want more.

"Hi, there. What's your name?" *His voice is deep and rich, like smooth syrup.*

In the most shocking move I've ever made, I take the beer bottle out of his hand and drink from it, never breaking eye contact. "Demi. And you are?"

I see the spark in his expression as he watches my lips wrap around the neck of the bottle. "You don't know who I am?"

"Should I?"

A grin spreads across his full lips. "I'm only the best athlete at this school, the football player who won you and everyone else a national championship last year."

Typically, I would think bragging like that is a turn off, a gross ego-builder. But this guy has me hypnotized, and I can see a bit of humor underneath his oversized sense of pride. And I genuinely don't know who he is, not being that into sports, and I think he gets off on that a little bit.

"Okay, best athlete, what's your name?"

His grin is even more cocky as he reaches out his hand. "Paxton Shaw, at your service."

The song changes and my body moves of its own accord. I grasp Paxton's hand, and I'm simultaneously shaking it and also pulling him up to dance with me.

That big body envelops me, his strong arms wrapping around my waist as his hands direct me in which way to sway. Our bodies mold together, the wrongness of how sexual I'm being feeling so right in this moment. I've never allowed myself to give in to something like this, to want this.

Paxton's mouth comes down on my neck as the next song thumps along the floor, and I gasp, not expecting the hot kiss on my skin. My legs become rubbery, my spine heats like wood melting under the flames. He's right there to hold me up, to continue his perusal of my collarbone as I feel the wetness pool between my thighs.

"Let's go upstairs," he whispers in my ear.

I've never been that kind of girl, have only seen this kind of scene in the movies. But I want it so badly, unlike I've ever wanted someone to touch me before. Almost like if he doesn't, I will die on the spot.

With our hands latched to each other, he leads me to the second floor of the house. I don't even know whose house this is, and yet two minutes later, I'm underneath a strange boy on a strange bed.

And loving every second of it.

The alcohol makes my brain fuzzy, and it seems like minutes pass that I don't remember. But I do remember the laughing, his hot mouth on my own lips, the way I ground into him, our clothes coming off.

Sex, for the two times I'd had it before, had always seemed like an act that a woman wouldn't enjoy but had to tolerate for a man.

Oh, how wrong I'd been.

The moment that Paxton had made me come, his hips thrusting into mine, I finally got it. I understood why men would do anything to get this, why women felt empowered and sexual and alive in the act of being intimate with another.

When he rolled off of me, both of us breathing heavy, I smiled up at the ceiling. Maybe, those times I'd given myself to other boys, it just hadn't been right. Maybe, it just needed to be with the right person. And at last, two years into this crazy life that college brought, I'd found the person I was meant to feel pleasure with.

The sound of a buckling belt had me stirring, sitting up on my elbows.

On the other side of the room, Paxton was fully dressed, and I felt a frown mark my lips. Where was he going? Surely, we could take a few more minutes to feel each other's skin, explore the dips and crevices of our bodies.

"I'll see you around, doll."

He winked at me, and then walked out the door, shutting it behind him.

Confusion and loneliness swept in. He hadn't kissed me, hadn't waited for me to dress and walked me back down. Hadn't even asked for my phone number.

It was the first time I'd ever acted on an impulse, went to bed with a stranger. And now I was faced with the cold, harsh truth that just like all the rest, he was a pig who wanted nothing more than to fuck me.

What a shame that every time I saw him after that night, amnesia set in where those feelings of abandonment were concerned.

Of course, I knew who Demi Rosen was.

And not because I'd done my research on her organization, the same I would for any business or charity who requested my time.

No, I knew exactly where I, and my hands, had been on that girl.

Well, I guess she was technically a woman now. And an absolute knockout at that. She'd matured since college, even though she'd been gorgeous then too. Her legs had gotten longer, if that was possible, her face a little leaner with sharp cheekbones and that mauve pout. Those eyes, impossibly big and framed by long black lashes, pierced you.

Demi had one of those bodies that seemed too good to be true. A tiny waist that gave way to a round, firm ass on bottom and tits that were each more than a handful on top. And even with those curves, she was almost rail-thin and model tall.

I'd known, going into this meeting, that she owned Wish Upon a Star. I'd had the exact same reaction to her as she'd had to me, but I'd had ample time to gape in the privacy of my own home. When I'd seen her picture on the website, my tongue had nearly fallen out of my mouth. The girl I'd fucked on and off for a few years in college, right in front of my eyes. My main booty call, some of the hottest sex I'd ever had, living right here in my new city.

I'd had the time to school my emotions before I saw her, which she clearly hadn't. Demi had no clue that I would be there. And when I had remained professional, for the sake of the family in that room, I'd seen the embarrassment creep over her face.

And for the millionth time where it concerned her, a small part of me died from guilt. I'd never done right by this girl, and when she'd all but stormed out of the conference room after the Gunter's left, I knew I had to go apologize.

But damn my half-aching cock if I didn't also selfishly want to see how she'd been.

I knock on her office door, and those dark brown eyes, the color of black coffee, take me in.

"Mr. Shaw, what can I do for you?" Demi's voice is clipped politeness.

I walk in, shutting her door behind me. I have a feeling her employees have no idea that we know each other, and I'm sure she doesn't want them to.

"I think we can drop the act, Demi."

It's strange, staring at the face of a person you once knew intimately. We were practically strangers now, and we hadn't known much about each other even back then.

Her face falters for just one moment, and then that fake smile is back. "It's nice seeing you again, Paxton. Thank you for doing this for the Gunter family."

I move farther into her office, a nice space decorated in white and gray, with framed portraits of London and two large vases filled with white roses. I wonder, in the back of my mind, if they're from a boyfriend or husband.

"Of course, he's a great kid. So, how have you been?" I want to sit down, but she looks apprehensive.

Flashes of when I used to make her moan, have her body writhing under me, assault my senses as I breathe in that familiar vanilla perfume. It's funny, no matter how many years have passed, that whenever I get a whiff of that scent, I think of Demi.

When I'd gotten the call eight years ago from my agent about the draft, I'd packed up my belongings at college and left two days later. I'd never looked back, hadn't bothered to say goodbye to her. I felt like a jackass for that move now.

I'd never returned the only two text messages she'd sent me, but then again all they'd said were, "Want to come over tonight?" and, "I heard you left campus." To the twenty-one-year-old douchebag that I was, those two sentences weren't really demanding or even remotely girlfriend-like, so I ignored them. Demi was part of my old life, and I was in training mode, and then traveling the country for games.

What I should have done was give the girl I'd been hooking up with for two years the decency of a goodbye. I should have at least told her I was leaving, instead of completely ghosting her.

But after those texts, she never tried to contact me again. Seeing her now, I feel the tension surrounding us. Maybe she hadn't cut things off as cleanly as I had, because it felt like there was a giant chip on her shoulder.

"I've been fine, thanks. How about yourself?" From her tone, I could tell she didn't really want to know.

I studied her, even though she was filing through papers on her desk in an attempt not to make eye contact. "I've been okay, moved back here about two months ago. A lot has changed in the city since those college days."

That makes Demi look at me, her mocha pools narrowing but the smile never leaving her lips. She's a well-trained professional, has the southern hospitality down pat. Someone who didn't know her would think she was being genuinely nice.

"Yes, it has. Well, we are looking forward to the game on Sunday. Again, thank you for doing this."

She's dismissing me, and I take the hint, not wanting to push her. Clearly, she doesn't want to talk to me, and I don't really blame her.

"Like I said, I'm happy to do it. I'll see you at the game. I'm number twenty, just like the old college days, if you didn't know."

Her grin screams pure bitch, but she just inclines her head.

I leave the Wish Upon a Star office feeling like I was just clocked in the head by an iceberg.

But, damn, was it good to see that fiery woman again.

PAXTON

Ten Years Ago

Mud is still caked under my fingernails, the only part I couldn't scrub out in the shower.

It was a hard fought game, but playing in the rain has always been my favorite. It makes football just a little bit tougher, running routes a little bit harder, the strain of your muscles just a little bit more painful.

Victory and exhaustion mix in my veins, and the team bus is a group of rowdy twenty-somethings sneaking shots behind the coaches back while getting ready to go wild once we roll back into campus. Saturday night and the parties and bars will be in full swing, just waiting for their kings to complete the chaos.

And while part of me wants to be bowed to, I also just want to go to bed. I scored three touchdowns tonight, practically carried the team on my back. My bones hurt, my feet are sore, and my head feels so heavy that I may just shut my eyes and fall asleep right here. I take another swig of whiskey from the flask being passed around, not that it will help my exhaustion.

No, I could go for a mighty fine blow job right now and then pass out.

Unlocking my cell phone, I pull up Demi's number and text her. We've been fucking for a few months now, and I know she's readily available any time I call.

I can see the hope in her eyes each time we finish, but I never broach the subject. I'm too busy for a girlfriend, and while she's a great lay, I'm not interested in more. My eyes are on the future, and a female will just tie me down.

It's almost too easy when she texts back within seconds saying she's free. Sometimes that's a turn off for me, a fact that I know is shitty but it's true all the same. Demi needs me way more than I need her ... but she's so damn hot in the sack that I can't give it up.

"Are you going to see your fuck buddy?" *Travis, my quarterback, takes the empty seat next to me.*

"Shit, that girl wants to be a wife. You haven't cut that off, yet?" *Darrell, our massive outside lineman, rolls his eyes at me.*

I give them both the finger. "Fuck you, guys. I'm not wifing anybody, and yeah, I'm going to get some pussy. Can't help it you're jealous that I'm getting consistent blow jobs from a fine-ass chick."

Darrell chuckles. "I can't argue that ... I am a little jealous. The tits on your girl ..."

He makes a sound like he's trying to imagine what Demi looks like naked. Not so secretly, I like that they envy me ... and that I'm the only guy she'll take it off for. Outside of what she does with me, she's the ultimate good girl ... another fact that makes it hard to break things off. It gets me harder than a steel pipe knowing that Demi is a lady in the streets and a freak in the sheets.

I flex my hands, cracking my knuckles. "Soak it up, fellas, and just know that when I snap my fingers, she comes crawling."

It was true. Twenty minutes later, I was sitting in my room in the house some of my teammates and I rented just off campus, when Demi came walking in. I'd texted, and she'd driven over at two in the morning. I didn't even have to make the effort to show up somewhere else to get my dick sucked.

"Hey, you." Demi was always shy when we first greeted each other, like she knew she should be ashamed for giving it up so easily but also not caring.

For one fleeting second, I felt bad for making her get out of bed in the chillier temperatures of fall in North Carolina. She is constantly driving over here in the middle of the night, alone, to my shitty room in my shitty house. I don't even have proper sheets, the king size threads too big on the queen frame. Most of the time, I make some excuse about why she can't stay over. And yet, here she is. I'm the lowest kind of scum, but at least I'm not lying to her about what I am. She clearly sees that I don't want to do anything remotely close to falling in love with her, and yet she continues to sleep with me.

I walked to her, my prick already half-cocked, my balls drawing up tight while the tingling sensation of arousal shot up my spine. "Hey, gorgeous."

Once my hands were wrapped around her waist, pulling down the leggings she donned, she warmed up a bit. "Great game, Pax. It looked so nasty out there, you sure you're okay?"

"I'm fine, but I could use a nurse if you want to tend to my wounds." I wink at her, my dirty mind in full force.

I push those leggings down past her hips, loving the rough feel of the calluses on my palms against her velvet skin. Using my lips on the spot just below her ear, I feel her preen like a cat in heat, pushing her hips against mine.

"You guys are only two games away from the championship, how exciting is that?" Demi pushes back, looking me in the eyes.

She's doing that thing again, the attempt to make a connection and talk. How come all girls want to talk? As if us guys are going to suddenly become one of their girlfriends and have a dish session. Demi tries to do this every so often. I think it's because she thinks that I'll suddenly become interested in something more with her than just sex.

Shutting her down, I cover her mouth with mine, plunging my tongue in deep, demonstrating the things I can do between her thighs. Sighing into my mouth, she gives way so easily, swayed by the skills I'm using as I nibble on her bottom lip.

Jutting my hips against her, Demi takes my not so subtle cue and reaches down into my sweatpants. Her small hand finds me, wrapping tight around the base and pumping just the way I like it. She makes sure to flick my head with her thumb on every upstroke, a little trick I taught her that makes my balls squeeze impossibly tighter and has me seeing sparks on the edge of my vision.

"That's it, baby. Get on the bed, ass up," I growl in her ear, needing to shove my cock between her velvety folds right now.

She does as she's told, knowing it will make her feel incredible. That round ass smiles up at me as I roll a condom on. If I asked, I could probably convince Demi to let me raw dog it ... but for now, I still wasn't that much of an asshole. I was extremely close, though.

I don't even take the time to finger her, or lick between those beautiful lips, because I'm horny and need to celebrate my victory tonight. Lining myself up to her, I groan when I sink in, her pussy gripping me tight.

This is how I like Demi best, beneath me, pliable, moaning. With every thrust, she pushes back on me. I wrap my fist in her hair and stroke how hard and how fast I want, never letting up. This is my situation to control, and it feels damn good to just be in this moment with no talking, just feeling.

I plow into her, not checking to see if she came, though by the sounds I'm pretty sure I've satisfied her. When my orgasm comes rocketing up from my balls, I still myself, feeling every blood vessel empty into the condom.

By the time I roll over, away from Demi, a glance at the clock reveals it's around three thirty in the morning. I want to fall asleep, stretch out by myself in my own bed. But, it's late, and I'm not that big of a dick that I'm going to send her out into the asscrack of dawn for a walk of shame.

"You can stay if you want." My tone conveys that I don't really want her to.

Those big brown eyes hold hope. "Are you sure?"

I turn on my side, looking back at her over my shoulder. "Yeah, it's late. It's cool."

I make sure not to touch her the entire rest of the night. And when I wake up around ten a.m., she's gone.

T he noise is deafening.

Towels of maroon and gold are waved in circles around almost every fans head, the bump of some hit pop song mixing with the cheers and chants of the home team.

My mouth waters, the scent of sausage and peppers, popcorn, beer and peanuts drifting on the wind. Everywhere you look, some kind of excitement is taking place. Whether it's the wide-eyed look of a child experiencing her first game, the mascot doing cartwheels down the sidelines, the coaches smacking their players on the shoulder pads, getting them pumped up.

Living in Charlotte for most of my adult life, the one thing I haven't done at all is attend a Cheetahs game. I think, after obsessing over Paxton's college career, football was one of the things I had to swear off when he left without so much as a goodbye the day he entered the draft. Anytime we had a wish that required attendance at a game, I sent Farrah. She never asked questions, but I knew that she understood that there was some kind of history there. So, while I knew a bunch of the players, and was friendly with many from hospital visits or signing days or charity dinners, I'd never shown up at a game.

"Demi Rosen, on the field! I never thought I'd see the day. And in heels no less." Greg Backus, the Cheetah's running back, stood in front of me in full uniform and pads.

Greg had tried to ask me out at least a dozen times. Not that he wasn't handsome, heck, I'm sure women in the Charlotte area would cut off their right hand to go out with him, but I stuck to my rule and always turned him down.

I peered down at my favorite Sam Edelman pumps. "A business woman always has to look the part. Plus, these heels are amazing."

His eyes heat. "Well, they look it. Are you going to let me take you out yet?"

"Hi, Demi. Nice to see you, again." At that exact moment, Paxton walks up.

It's bad enough I have to see the jerk who stomped on my heart, but does he have to be so freaking gorgeous? Paxton looks like Thor, before the Thor movies even existed. With an earring. If you've never been with a guy with an earring, you're missing the boat. It's a surprisingly huge turn on.

"Paxton." I nod my head.

"Hey, don't give the new guy all the attention. Remember who was here first." Greg winks at me before running down the sideline to get his ankle taped.

Paxton narrows his eyes at Greg's retreating back, and I want to slap him. He has absolutely no claim over me, not anymore.

But clearly, he remembers what we were to each other. He'd made that known when he came into my office and tried to have a jovial conversation. I'm not interested in any of that, and I hope I got that message across. I'm gritting my teeth and bearing this until today is over and I never have to be in the same room as Paxton Shaw again.

"Miss Demi, look at my jersey!" Ryan runs over to me, his bald scalp covered by a Cheetahs hat, a jersey signed by all the players hanging down to his knees.

"That is too cool, you're one lucky kid to get one of those. And to have so many players look up to you. I heard you scored a touchdown on Connor Ike before!"

Ryan and his family had gotten to spend most of this week's practice days, and the warm-ups hours before today's game, with the team. They'd included him in drills, throwing passes, film watching, and running through today's play calls. I'd laid this all out with Harry, the public relations rep we usually dealt with.

"I did, and kicked the extra point! And now they gave me a headset. Pax is really awesome." He's missing one of his front teeth, and my God is he adorable.

We're down on the sidelines, where we'll stay for the entirety of the game. The staff gave him an official earpiece, so he can hear all of the plays as they're being called.

And yes, Paxton had been really sweet with him. I'm not sure why I'm surprised, he's clearly practiced at media training being in the league for so long. But I silently thanked him for being so good to Ryan. He hadn't left his side since day one of meeting the little boy, and I knew that in the long run, Ryan would remember and cherish this wish for the rest of his life.

Bitterness and upset have a ball of emotion clogging my throat. The rest of his life. That may not be long. Fuck this fucking disease, and the fact that it took children so young.

"Buddy, watch for my first touchdown, I'm coming to give that ball right to you." Pax ruffles Ryan's hat.

"And now, your North Carolina Cheetahs!" The voice booming on the sound system drowns out my thoughts.

The crowd goes insane as the rest of the team runs out of the tunnel, and the players on the sideline wave to the crowd or jump up and down, getting pumped up.

Even when times were best between Paxton and me, a six month stretch during my junior year where we made a semi-go of being exclusive, he hadn't invited me to attend a game as his girlfriend. One of my biggest dreams was to sit in the family section, next to the other girls wearing their boyfriend's number, known by all the families as Pax's girl.

But he never gave me that, and looking back now, my heart aches with sadness for the girl too insecure to dump his loser ass and get rid of the guy who treated me like shit. Because that was what he did, everyone saw it. My friends, Chelsea especially, would berate me for staying in any Saturday night the football team had a game, my eyes glued to the television watching Paxton score touchdowns.

So, when, on the fourth drive of the game, Pax soars through the air into the end zone, my heart leaps. I don't want it to, but old habits die hard.

He runs down the sideline to where Ryan is and thrusts the point-scoring ball into his hands before lifting him up on his shoulders. The video board in the stadium shows the two of them cheering, and the crowd goes wild for this little boy who, in this moment, can forget all about the illness plaguing him.

As soon as it's socially acceptable to leave the game, I bolt. Another minute inside that stadium and all of the carefully constructed walls I'd used to steel myself against my past would come crumbling down.

8

DEMI

"Tell me I did not just watch what I thought I did." Chelsea's voice comes in over the bluetooth in my car. "Hi to you too, Chels."

"Don't bullshit me, Demi Rachel. You can't stand next to the Axis of Evil and just think your best friend is not going to call you to see if you were scorched standing that close to Hades."

I roll my eyes. "You're being dramatic. I'm a professional, this was part of my job. I'm fine."

The doubt rings in her tone. "I don't buy it. It took you years to get over that asshole. I know, I was there. I had to talk you down multiple times."

Memories of crying silently into my pillow plague me, but I push them to the back of my brain. "I'm fine, Chels, really. I'm a thirty year old woman with her own business, I'm mature enough to be able to see a former flame and live to tell about it."

I wind my car through downtown, passing the skyscrapers and heading towards my condo in Davidson, a suburb just outside the city.

Silence follows for a few seconds before she speaks again.

"Okay, I believe you. But I need details. How the hell did this happen?"

I sigh and tell her about Ryan, and his wish, and how hands on Paxton has been. It was actually kind of sweet watching them together.

I scold myself for thinking fondly of him at the same time that Chelsea does. "So he's helping out a sick kid ... still doesn't make him a good person. In fact, I can still feel the rage boiling in my gut when I think about the prick."

I have to laugh, because damn if she isn't the best friend ever. We talk for the rest of my twenty five minute car ride, about her patients at the dentist office she works at as a hygienist. About my parents and hers, about the mouse she's been trying to catch in her apartment. When we hang up, promising to text each other during *Dancing with the Stars,* I'm left with the sense of loneliness I usually am when I say goodbye to Chelsea.

She decided to move home after college, electing not to stay in Charlotte, the city we'd attended college in. Unlike me, she wanted to be close to home and her family in Connecticut. And not that I didn't love my parents or where I grew up, but I felt the need to branch out. And if I'd gone back to Queens, I would have fallen into the same old rhythm.

As the bustle of the city melts away behind me, I can feel the tenseness in my shoulders unwind. I bought a condo in the cute neighborhood of Davidson about two years ago, wanting to plant some roots and get out of the city.

It was the best decision I ever made. It is my paradise, the two floor white brick abode with an attached garage. I painted it in neutral tones, doing all of the fix ups myself for months and on the weekends. In the summer, I sit on my back patio and drink iced tea with my Kindle. In the winter, I light my wood-burning fireplace and snuggle up with a glass of wine.

And then of course, there is Maya.

My golden retriever runs to greet me as soon as I push open the door, not even allowing me to get the keys out of the lock before she's twirling at my feet, wanting to go out.

"Hi, sweet pea!" I bend down, dropping my bag on the floor and kicking my heels off at the same time I nuzzle into her fur.

Maya is the only one I need to live with. She doesn't nag me for getting my nails done twice a month, or keep the television turned to ESPN twenty-four seven, or need constant reassurance about the size of her ego.

No, she is perfectly happy to sit next to me on the couch, being petted and occasionally fed some human food. Maya occupied the other side of my queen size, and delighted in walks in the park on weekend mornings. She was my child, my confidant, and the one I looked forward to coming home to.

"Who is the best girl in the world?" I cooed at her as I put her leash on to take her out.

Twilight is setting in, the world both going dark and lighting up simultaneously. I may be a hustler during the day, but nighttime has always been my favorite. A sense of mystery, the shadows allowing us to feel something that the daytime prohibits. The moon and it's tapestry of stars, artwork put there for our perusal. The sense of relaxation that comes with the winding down of a day.

But the one thing I despise about the hours after seven p.m. is the loneliness. The stark feeling of being by myself sets in fast when the sun goes down.

9

Being a professional athlete is both a blessing and curse. On the blessing side, I get to go to a job I love passionately every single day. I also get paid a hell of a lot of money to do it. I'm damn good, and being a football player fulfills my fiercely competitive nature.

But it isn't all hot girls, fast cars, and piles of cash. Athletes at this level work fucking hard. Cutting food out of our diets, forgoing families because it's just too tough to form attachments when you're on the road this much. Keeping your ear to the ground, wondering every second if you're going to get benched or cut.

And then there is the physical demands it puts on you. I work out seven days a week, sometimes three or four hours a day. And on top of that the massage and physical therapy I do, and keeping my body in shape is basically a second full-time job.

That's why I'm in Freedom Park, getting ready to sweat like a beast with one of my teammates.

"What have you been doing in your spare time around Charlotte, my dude? Good to be back?" Connor fist bumps me and begins to stretch, both of us waiting for Anthony.

He's one of the older guys on the team, a cornerback who I train with a lot since our positions are opposites on offense and defense. An easy going southern gentlemen from Tennessee, Connor is just good to talk to and have a beer with. He's confident without being cocky, which is a rare gem in this league and frankly the only kind of player I want to surround myself with these days. I'm too old to kick it with the newbies trying to prove something.

"Not much, man ... just trying to hit all of the amazing restaurants that have popped up since I left. And I'm working with Wish Upon a Star, they paired me up with the Gunter family, you might have seen Ryan on the sidelines at last week's game?"

"Oh, yeah, awesome kid. So sad, though, man ... why does life have to be such a cold bitch? And speaking of cold, but sexy as hell, bitches, that's why Demi Rosen was down on the field on Sunday." He nodded as he bent over to touch his toes, stretching his hamstrings.

"You know Demi?" I try not to look too eager.

Anthony walks up as Connor continues. "Man, everyone knows Demi. The finest lady in the entire city of Charlotte, and she's locked up tighter than a clam protecting its prized pearl."

"What does that mean?" I stretch an arm over my head.

"What're we talking about?" Anthony shakes my hand and nods at Connor.

"Demi ... Shaw here just met her for the first time while taking on a wish kid."

Anthony begins to unpack his bag on the grass; a few weights, some resistance bands, stopwatch and mats. "Oh, she's great, really does a wonderful job for those families. And my wife is just crazy about her. But yeah ... she is kind of cold to newcomers. If you're thinking what every other guy in the locker room usually considers when it comes to Demi, I'd drop that idea now. According to Lucy, she doesn't date."

Hmm, so she was single. But apparently, liked to stay that way. Is it wrong that I get just a little excited that the flowers in her office weren't from another man?

"Damn shame too, that girl is wife material." Connor shakes his head.

Once we're done stretching, Anthony details the circuit training we're going to be doing, each round of reps broken up by two minutes of full-out suicide sprints in this grass. We start, the workout surprisingly intense for being done in a sunny park. It's nice to get out of the weight room, I rarely do workouts like this nowadays.

Around the third time I cut and turn to sprint and touch the line during suicide drills, a sharp pain rockets through my knee.

"Fuck!" I let up, hopping up and down as one does when pain radiates through your leg.

"You okay?" Anthony rushes over, his whistle still in hand. I think he's a strength coach and trainer because he loves it, but I also think he secretly loves to be a slave driver.

Connor stops too, and I hate the sympathetic looks they're both giving me. I stand there, shaking off my knee and trying to put pressure on it. It feels okay, not like anything popped, but I'm cautious.

"Yeah, just a little sore. My old bones aren't what they used to be." Except that it's not just sore.

If I'm being truthful with myself, this is probably my last season. I've denied it for as long as I can ... but dammit, I can't even run a couple of sprint drills. With two rings already in the safe in my house, I was hoping to add a third before I was put out to pasture and retirement. It has to happen this season, or I

don't think I'll be able to stand up on that winner's podium ever
again.

"Take it easy, Shaw, I don't need you tearing something else
on my watch." Anthony's gaze is suspicious, and he probably
knows I'm downplaying the pain.

I nod, promising to do so. But all three of us know it's now or
never, and I'm sacrificing my body in whatever ways necessary to
add that final victory to my personal record sheet.

———

One of the best things about the place that Cheetah's
management set me up with is the rooftop deck.

Most guys in my profession are happy at a loud
sports bar, on the golf course, or partying in some VIP nightclub.
But me? I'm a "sit and watch the stars" kind of guy if there ever
was one. Growing up in the small wharf town my parents settled
in in Rhode Island, my brother and I established a routine from
an early age.

Almost every night after dinner, we'd take our lawn chairs
and set them up on the dock behind our house, the water occu-
pying the small inlet of the Atlantic Ocean we lived on lapping
at the tiny beach of our property. We'd sit there, as kids drink
apple juice, and shoot the shit as the stars lit up the sky. Over the
years, friends were added, and when high school and college hit,
so was alcohol. But after everyone left, and it was just me and
him or another few close friends, we'd sit on those lawn chairs
and talk about life.

Sitting up on the roof deck of my apartment now, watching
the stars twinkle as I sip from a bottle of beer, only reminds me
of one thing.

My parents at home on the shores of Rhode Island.

I hope that they're doing the same thing right now, sitting up there among the stars. I hope they're not in pain. That they are hand in hand looking down on me as I stare up thinking about them.

Five years ago, their lives were taken way too early by the same sea that we sat by as kids. They shouldn't have gone out that day, the weather report had been spotty at best. But Mom was feeling like an afternoon sailboat ride, and Dad never could say no to her.

When the coast guard found their boat, they told us that our parents didn't stand a chance against the storm. The waves were too great, and even though my father had been an expert boatsman, there was nothing he could have done.

Having to identify your parent's bodies ... that was a nightmare you never got out of your head.

Their deaths changed me as a person. Where I was once social, I tended to stick to small groups or simply be alone nowadays. Partying and women held no interest for me anymore, and it had been a long while since I'd taken a female to bed. I kicked myself every day for not giving my parents what they wanted most; me, settled and happy with a family. Hell, how they had wanted a grandchild to dote over.

When the sea had taken my parents, it had also taken my ego. A little bit of my spark. It made me realize, even if I'd had a great relationship with my mother and father, just how important spending time with family was. All of the other stuff was just minutiae. It meant nothing if you didn't have people in your life that you loved.

And so, as I gaze up at the many galaxies, the noises of Charlotte after dark down below me on the street, I can't help but regret not finding the time to fill my life with more people I loved.

10

Ryan cringes as the needle goes into his arm, turning his little face away, but I watch the entire time.

The room I sit in, in the Charlotte Children's Hospital, is filled with kids under the age of twelve receiving chemotherapy treatments. I want to fucking scream, my internal rage meter so high that I have to dig my nails into my palms as my hands form fists.

Who the fuck made it possible that innocent children could get diagnosed with cancer? It should be illegal, immoral, impossible. I want to grab these doctors by the coat and demand a cure.

But, knowing none of that will help, I just sit beside Ryan and discuss passing plays while holding his hand, the poison dripping into his veins.

Before my parent's accident, I probably would have just been a one and done kind of guy. Let the kid come to a game, escort him around, give him a jersey. But ... that was the last half of my life. This was a new half, sliced in two by the definitive event of their passing.

If seeing me, talking to me, hanging out with me, was going

to make Ryan feel better, then I was going to spend every spare minute doing that for him. This kid, so brave and spunky, deserved whatever he wanted for having to go through this shit. And I was going to give whatever that was to him. I sure as hell had the money, and I had the time. And besides, he was one awesome little dude.

"Want to play Go Fish?" Ryan moves the deck of cards his mom put on the table between us.

"Are you going to let me win? Because if so, I'm not sure I want to play," I tease him.

He giggles. "Yeah right, I'm gonna kick your butt!"

I wink at him. "I was hoping you'd say that."

We play a couple of hands, Ryan wincing every so often and having to pause because he feels nauseous.

About an hour into sitting with him, Demi walks through the door.

And stops completely short when she sees me. "Oh, I didn't realize ... I didn't know you'd be here ... I can come back ..."

She's lost her head seeing me here, of that I'm sure. It makes me sad but amuses me. She has no idea how to act around the asshole who left without so much as a goodbye. But she's flustered, which means she still feels something for me. Even if it's deep hatred.

Her hair is always the first thing I remember, falling down her back in long golden brown waves. It used to smell like sugar cookies. She's dressed down in jeans and a simple long sleeve. Even though she looks like a hot librarian in that business wear I've seen her in twice now, I find I like her even better like this. She's more approachable than the formidable persona she now embodies as the CEO of Wish Upon a Star.

Yeah, I looked her up before and after working with her. Her company is one of the most successful businesses in all of Charlotte, and the second most successful nonprofit that helps provide wish fulfillment to sick kids. She built it on her own back, and she takes crap from no one, while still maintaining that cheery disposition. Seriously, that was a line written about her in an article.

"Hey, Demi! Want to come play Go Fish with us?" Luckily, the seven-year-old sitting next to me doesn't understand the emotions flying between her and me.

That makes her snap out of the death stare she's currently giving me. "Of course!"

For the duration of Ryan's treatment, the three of us play cards, and Demi teaches Ryan how to play poker. By the end of it, he's hustling us both. It's funny, I had no idea she knew how to play poker that well.

Then again, I don't really know a thing about her now.

Ryan falls asleep after, and the nurses let us know that we should probably let him rest.

We walk out into the hospital hallway, awkwardly moseying side by side.

"So, bye," Demi says at the same time I ask, "Would you like to grab some dinner?"

The shock on her face at me proposing to have a meal together is palpable.

"Why would we have dinner together?" The malice in her tone has me taking a step back.

I hold out a hand. "Look, Demi, I know what an asshole I was back then. And I'm really sorry for that. I've thought about calling you a hundred times in the last decade or so to apologize."

"What a surprise that you didn't." Sarcasm drips from her tongue.

Damn. I realize I did a number on this girl. But I didn't realize she'd still be hating me for it. Not that I can blame her.

"I know you won't believe me, but I've changed. Life hasn't been as kind to me as it was when we were in college."

Demi looks away, crossing her arms over her chest. "Says the professional football player who makes millions a year."

"Money doesn't buy you happiness, of that I'm sure," I mutter.

That makes her gaze swing back to mine, those big brown eyes searching my soul.

"Have dinner with me. Let me make at least a small portion of what I did up to you." I'm acutely aware that I'm begging.

I watch as she fights with herself internally, but finally she blows out a big sigh. "Fine. But I'm picking the place."

Demi chooses an Italian fusion bistro with beer on tap from Sicily and flatbread pizza that smells like heaven. Dinner is ... awkward at best. I ask questions mostly, and she gives me one-word answers. At times, there are such painful silent gaps that I cringe and stuff way too much bread in my mouth. I'm going to pay in cardio workouts for a week after consuming this many carbs.

Our dessert comes, a piece of cobbler for me and a cappuccino for her. I never could say no to southern desserts, and I might as well indulge. I'm old and washed up now anyway, if you listen to the reporters.

"You never told me why you do what you do." I try to stay on a neutral topic, show interest.

Because I may have been a jerk back then, but I'm very interested in getting to know her now.

Demi considers me, and I'm worried she's just going to phone in her answer. But then she speaks some of the most inspiring words I've ever heard. "I think of each one of these children as a precious star. One whose life on earth may be short, but their time floating around that great, big mystical universe is far from over. They may be burning out for us, we may soon be unable to see their shine, but they will always be here, looking over us when the night sky comes to life."

And that's when I realize that I'm such a fucking fool. Have been one for ten years. Because I never got to truly know Demi, and there is clearly so much more to this woman than I ever allowed myself to learn.

I'm a goddamn moron, and regret and self-hatred kick me in the gut. How could I have been so blind to look past a woman who would have that kind of outlook on death? Who would willingly get to know innocent children who were fighting the most horrible of diseases. Most people would throw them a sympathetic look and keep going, unable to cope with the sheer sadness their lives hold.

But she ... she sits with them at treatments long after their wishes are fulfilled. I have a feeling she's constantly checking up on her past families, as well as meeting new ones to make their children's dreams come true.

And the way she describes death ... well, if it's anything like that then I hope my parents got to experience it the way she thinks of it.

"That's ... that's beautiful." I have to swallow down my emotion.

Demi looks at me, her expression guarded as if she's wondering if I'm mocking her. But, I'm not. We haven't seen each other for eight years, and while the accident was reported on since I was already famous when it happened, there is a good chance she has no idea that my parents died.

Honestly, I never opened up enough to even tell her much

about them. I was too busy calling her at three in the morning for a quick fuck.

"I'm sorry that we never talked more, back then. I was an idiot college kid, and I should have treated you better. We really could have gotten to know each other."

I'm surprised when Demi chuckles, but when I meet her eyes, they aren't sweet. They're cutting, bitter, scrutinizing.

"I did know you, Paxton. Your birthday is March eleventh, you grew up in Rhode Island and played every sport under the sun before landing on football. I think you have one brother, although you never talked about your family much. You prefer Sam Adams over any other beer, can kick the crap out of anyone in a karaoke competition, and are actually quite good at math even though you'd never admit that to your buddies back in the day. You washed your sheets in Tide only, I'm not sure why, but it was the only detergent ever in your closet. You like Crest toothpaste and hate cologne unless it's so mild you can barely smell it. I did know you; I took any morsel you were willing to disclose and stored it away just in case someday you decided to want me for real. Then I'd be able to do all of those girlfriend things for you, know the things partners were supposed to."

Shock and agony ring out in my veins ... I'm a fucking prick. I go to apologize profusely, but she cuts me off.

"Don't bother, it's about ten years too late. Just know that I did know you, and you couldn't bother to even learn my middle name."

With that, she gets up from the table and turns on her heel. A second later, she's marching back. Without a word, she throws a few twenty-dollar bills on the table.

That burns. Because this woman thinks so lowly of me that she won't even let me buy her dinner to make up for the years of mistreatment I made her endure.

11

W hy had I done that?

Eight years. Eight perfectly fine years, I'd gone without an utterance of his name. It had been at least three since I'd stopped picturing his face at least once a day. I was good, I was stable.

And then I had to go and be a masochist, sharing a meal with him and melting when he talked. I could feel myself slipping, right there in between our entrees and dessert. That's why I had to put him in his place, to put my head back on straight.

Because what I'd said was true. I had studied him, catalogued every piece of information he'd been willing to give me. I knew him inside out. And he hadn't known me, not one bit.

He'd been the reason I couldn't fall in love with anyone else, not when I'd been so rejected for so long by the one man I'd loved blindly. Even when someone had loved me faithfully, with all of my flaws, I couldn't give enough to make it work.

I thought about Zachary ... something I hadn't done in a while. four years ago, when my meddling yenta of a mother couldn't stand me not bringing someone to Hanukkah anymore, my parents set me up with the son of a woman from their synagogue.

He was Jewish, tall, dark and handsome, he had a good job in the restaurant sector. Zach was charming and attentive, just the kind of guy I needed. He opened doors, made dinner, sent me flowers to the office.

So, when he popped the question a year into us dating, I'd said yes. Even though I hadn't felt it with my full heart, my head knew that this was good for me. That he'd make a good husband, that I didn't have to be madly in love to be content.

Only ... when my mother had come over two weeks later armed with wedding magazines, veil samples and the number for the best bakery in town ... I knew it would never work. My walls were still up, I still couldn't *feel* a thing. And I wasn't as horrible of a person as Paxton Shaw, I would never bind someone to me forever who I couldn't love equally. I knew what a horrible fate that was.

So why had I gone to dinner with Paxton last night? I knew what kind of person he was, and yet I was still under his spell, all these years later.

We were nothing more than a flash in the pan. A few hot hours of mind-bending sex and some pillow talk. He made me shake like no one else could, or ever had. But that's the thing about the guy who makes you feel the best kind of high possible; he's never the committing type. You don't fall in love with the boy who makes you feel like your throat is the new Sahara Desert, or the one who has you sneaking out at all hours of the night. No, you settle down with the calm, respectable, man. The one who knows a thing or two about priorities and building a life. That's who you promise yourself to in the long run.

But I'd had stable, and I'd thrown it away. Apparently, no matter how hard I denied it, my heart wanted insanity.

It's why I was sitting in this goddamn box, high up in the

Cheetahs stadium, pretending I wasn't trying to sneak a glance at him down on the field.

"Try the coconut shrimp, they're delicious." Gina comes over with a plate stacked high with finger foods.

"You're a bottomless pit. If I ate that, I'd have to go to like, ten cycling classes." Farrah rolls her eyes and sips the glass of Chardonnay in her hand.

Farrah was a workout fiend. While I enjoyed a good run here and there, she spent every single morning in the most intense workout classes the city offered. And then there was Gina, who was ninety pounds soaking wet and could scarf down whatever she wanted.

I was somewhere in the middle.

I'm still not sure why I agreed to come to this game, although it would have been rude to refuse tickets that the Cheetahs general manager had sent personally after all of the good press we brought to the team from Ryan Gunter's wish.

And I wanted to prove to myself that having my ex-fling, because he never let me call him boyfriend, in *my* city was not going to limit where I could go inside of it.

The Cheetahs were winning fourteen to three in the third quarter, and I had spent the game alternating from sipping glasses of the delicious Cabernet they had at the free bar and trying to seem disinterested on what was happening down on the field.

But it was difficult. Watching Paxton on the field was something akin to a work of art. Although ... he wasn't as graceful in his movements as he once was. How funny, it had been years since I'd seen him on the football field, and yet I still noticed that something was off. Don't get me wrong, he was still very talented ... but some of that dazzle that he used to bring was burnt out.

"I'm surprised he is even playing this year. He's so old, and

after tearing his MCL, everyone said he wouldn't come back."
Gina is so blunt as she sits down next to me with a new plate.

"He tore his MCL?" Like I said, I'd avoided following his
career whatsoever.

Farrah tilts her head to the side. "It was only like, the biggest
story in sports last season."

I shrug, trying to feign ignorance. "You guys know I'm not
big into sports. I think the last time I turned on ESPN, it was to
watch Tim Tebow run shirtless through training camp."

"God, he was so sexy. Pretty dense, but so sexy." Farrah sighs.

"You're a football snob. Branch out, discover the world of
Bryce Harper's nude photos for the Body Issue." Gina scoffs at
our raven-haired coworker.

"Hey, nudity is nudity, and I'm A-OK with all of it." Farrah
clinks her glass to mine, even though I'm not a part of this
ridiculous discussion.

"But anyways, yeah, tore it right in two. He had to be carted
off the field, crying. Only other time the fans have seen him that
emotional is when he scored that touchdown the day after his
parents died in that accident. It was horrible, but he played his
best game the next day." Gina shakes her head, sadness in her
eyes.

"What?" Shock paralyzes me. "His parents died?"

Farrah nods. "Oh, it was awful, I remember the photos from
the funeral on ESPN. They died on their sailboat in an unex-
pected storm near their home. They died on a Saturday, and
there was so much speculation whether Paxton would play the
next day ... especially since the game had playoff implications.
But he did. Ended up scoring three touchdowns. After the game,
he refused media interviews but was seen kneeling, crying, in
the end zone when everyone went into the locker room."

Goose bumps break out all over my skin. How had I not
known that his parents had died? Sure, he'd never let me meet

them, but I'd seen pictures, heard him talk about them on occasion. Hell, we were involved for two years, I knew about his family. Immediately, I felt like a horrible person.

I swallow the lump of bile in my throat and try to remain neutral. "How long ago was that?"

Gina considers it, putting a finger to her chin. "About five years? Yeah, must have been, because I watched the game with some jackass fraternity brother who ended up asking if we could have a threesome that night."

Farrah chuckles. "Ah, such a prude. You should have taken him up on it. Three is better than two."

"Thank you, Dr. Sex Addict." Gina rolls her eyes. "But yeah, he's never really been the same since. People say he's a better athlete, but he's like a machine. No more passion in him."

For the rest of the game, I ruminate over what Gina has said. I've spent the past eight years changing, but maybe so has Paxton. I never considered that events happened in his life to make him a different person, like he'd said when he asked me to dinner.

Someone in the Cheetahs front office asks if we want to go down on the field for the end of the game, and the girls squeal their excited yeses. I follow, still in a trance about Paxton's parents. I should have sent flowers or something. Sent a card at least. Perhaps I could let him know now how sorry I was.

The game ends with a victorious win for the home team, and we watch as the players high five and slap asses. I spot Paxton across the field, pulling off his helmet and revealing his sweaty, golden hair. How is it possible that even after more than two hours of fighting tooth and nail for a win, he looks edible?

But now I consider him in a different light. I know what it's like to lose one of the closest people to you, how your world turns on its axis and you're never quite the same. What must it have been like to lose two people, especially the ones who brought you into this world?

I'm about to walk over, show him some kind of friendliness after I was so cold to him.

Except, when I'm about three feet away, a reporter walks up to him with a tape recorder and notebook. Blonde, big chested, in a tight red dress that looks so out of place in this venue. She's batting her lashes and throwing her hair over her shoulder.

And Paxton is smiling back at her, their body language flirty.

They say that an amputee can still feel phantom pain, even after their limb is gone.

That's what it's like watching Paxton talk to this reporter, her hand on his arm. It sends me flashing back to one of the most miserable times in my life. When despair and dejection were my two best friends.

Nine Years Ago

Another Saturday night, another party at some shitty house with shitty keg beer.

My friends are having a blast, meeting new guys or playing drinking games. They're letting loose, like normal girls in their junior year. After a week full of stressful classes and exams, I should be doing the same.

But I can't.

Because I've been watching Paxton grind on a busty redhead for the last hour and a half.

I down another shot of vodka that someone pours and leaves on the counter, making it my fifth. My bones are jello, my heart is smashed to a thousand pieces, and I feel like I might throw up from dejection any second.

We had been sleeping together for over a year now, late night calls and sneaking around was our specialty. Not that I wanted it to be, but any time I broached the conversation of becoming more, Pax had the best counters to snake out of the conversation.

He'd charm his way out with talk that tricked me, manipulating *his way around the subject without giving a straight answer. Or he would kiss me, using his talents to shut me up and get me off. Or he would explain about his future and football, and I'd be dumb enough to fall for that answer again.*

When Pax sees me on campus, he either waves or smiles, but never comes up to walk with me or have a conversation. Usually, he's always flanked by a buddy or two, ever the social butterfly. That person who is with him will always smirk, as if they know who I am.

I get the distinct feeling his friends talk about me behind my back, that they know I'm the poor desperate girl that Pax keeps in a drawer and takes out when he feels like playing with her.

Shame burns at the base of my neck, and tears well up in the corners of my eyes. Why does he do this to me? Deep down, I know how he truly is, even if no one else sees it. In those moments when we lay next to each other after sex, our heads on the pillows, talking about nonsense ... that is who Paxton Shaw truly is.

But the question I should really be asking myself is, why do I stay? Why do I allow myself to be emotionally abused like this?

Especially when he's across the room, using his lips to explore that girl's collar bone. I've heard rumors of him going home, mostly from Chelsea who wants me to ditch him so she can cut off his penis. Or at least that's what she always tells me. I had never believed her, being too blind for my own good when it came to him.

But now ... I wanted to throw things. Smash plates. Play Boyz II Men on repeat while eating ice cream and watching chick flicks starring Gerard Butler.

Before I know what I'm doing, my feet are marching me across the room.

"Jackass!" I get up in their space, screaming at Pax.

A few drunk students around us giggle at the girl being overdramatic at a party. The redhead Pax has been mauling glances up, her eyes glassy and confused.

"Excuse me?" Her tone is rude and aggressive.

Pax is the only one staring at me like I'm an injured deer. "Demi, go home. You're drunk. Go find Chelsea."

He's talking to me like I'm a five-year-old, like he doesn't know me at all. Like he pities me.

"Fuck you, Pax." My words are slurred and angry.

"Is this your girlfriend?" Redhead backs away from him.

"No," Pax says at the same time I laugh my head off.

"Whatever this is, I'm not getting involved in drama." She puts her hand up to him and then melts away into the crowd.

"Fucking Christ, Demi!" He throws his hands up, fury painted all over his face.

I cower, embarrassed about what I just did but also feeling desperate and small. Pax grabs my elbow and leads me outside, into the darkest part of the yard where no one can hear us. To others, we look like a couple in the midst of a fight. But I know that he's about to shatter my heart into a million more pieces.

Why am I a glutton for punishment?

"What the hell was that? I thought we agreed, we have a good time when we're together, and we have fun separate when we're out."

I poke him in the chest, all of the wrongs he's committed against me making me go out of my mind. "No, you agreed to that! You just want to have your cake and eat other's cake too, you piece of shit!"

Pax runs his hands through his shaggy blond hair. "Demi ... you aren't my girlfriend. We fuck sometimes. Shit, I knew this might happen. I knew you'd probably catch feelings."

He says this matter of factly, like I'm some sort of emotional female and he isn't at fault for any of this. I can practically hear the ventricles of my heart cracking under his fist, tears falling freely from my eyes.

"You are an asshole. You lead me on, build me up and act like we're ... like we could be something. Do you feel anything for me? I want a straight answer this time."

I'm shaking, so mad and so hurt that I can't see straight.

Pax looks at me, more pity in his eyes. "I don't know what to tell you, Demi—"

The alcohol gets the best of me, I pull my hand back, and smack him across the face. The sound reverberates under the trees, out of the sight of anyone else. Even when we fight, no one is present to see it. Our entire relationship takes place in the shadows.

We stare at each other, and I can't believe I had the gaul to do that.

I run, in the opposite direction, hating the person who would beg for a boy's attention and get so worked up that I'd resort to physical violence.

Two days later, when he texts me to apologize, I end up in his bed at one a.m.

13

I knew she was up there, watching me down on that field.

It fueled me, knowing that somewhere within the Cheetahs stadium, Demi was cheering for me. Hopefully. Actually, she was probably rooting for me to get tackled by a three-hundred pound linebacker. But that was besides the point. I hadn't felt the need to impress anyone in a very long time, and it almost made me feel like the cocky teen I once was. The one who jogged out under those Friday night lights for his hometown to see.

Except when I finally caught up with her employees in the family slash friends suite after the game, where the players met the people who'd come to the game for them, she wasn't there.

"Farrah, right?" I pointed at the girl I thought was her number two at Wish Upon a Star.

The girl, who looked a little bit like a goth version of Olivia Munn, did a double take when I approached her. "Um ... yeah."

"Hi. Paxton." I wave. "I think we met at your office?"

The girl standing next to her, a petite blond who looked a lot younger than either of us, gaped at me. "You did. I mean, you met her. You met both of us. We both work there."

"Down, Sparky." Farrah rolls her eyes. "This is Gina."

I wave at Gina, too. "Did Demi come with you?"

A look of ... something passes between them. "Yeah, she did. Why?"

"Do you know where she is?" I'm being weird, I know it. But I don't have to explain myself.

"She left a few minutes ago. Had to get home to feed her dog." Farrah looks at me with questions in her eyes.

"Thanks for coming." I smile, and quickly turn around.

Taking the player exits to the parking lot, I beat half of the traffic to get outside. I know what lot VIP pass holders get to park in, and I had to reach it before Demi could leave. This was neutral ground technically, I couldn't just drive to her house or her office. She'd feel bombarded, and she didn't want to talk to me as it was.

"Demi!" I shout, seeing her across the parking lot.

She's dressed down in jeans and a simple shirt, but she still has heels on and my cock is stirring like a caged tiger as I near her. Jesus, I guess it slipped my mind all these years just how fucking *beautiful* she is. All long legs and poise, I want to break that professional facade all the way down.

What the fuck was wrong with twenty-something me? I hadn't known what I'd had right in front of me.

Almond-colored hair whipped through the air as she turned her head, and I knew from the look on her face that she knew my voice. And from the look on said face, she wasn't pleased to find me walking toward her.

"Paxton." It wasn't a friendly greeting, but it wasn't a slap and I counted my blessings.

"Did you enjoy the game?" I'm standing too close when I reach her, but she can't back up because the car is behind her back.

"I did, thank you. I have to go." She wants nothing to do with me.

"Would you like to grab some dinner with me?" I'm shameless, but it's hard not to be around her now.

Demi tilts her head to the side, her eyes giving nothing away. "No, thank you. I have a prior engagement."

I catch the car door as she tries to open it and get in. "What, letting your dog out?"

She scowls. "Who told you that?"

I shake my head. "Doesn't matter, but Fido can wait. Come have dinner with me?"

"Because it went *so* well the last time." She mutters, and then her eyes go wide, like she didn't mean to say it out loud.

I like when Demi goes off script. All of the times I've been around her in the last couple of weeks, she seems untouchable, icy. It dawns on me that I may be the cause of some of that, and guilt is a cold bastard.

"I admit, it didn't go well, but I owe you. I've been an asshole, I know that. And it will give us a chance to talk about ..." I point between us. "Us."

Demi rolls her eyes and tries to get in the car again. A thought must permeate her brain, because she whips back around, and fury rolls off of her.

"Why do you assume I want to pursue anything between us? I have lived my life for eight whole years without ever seeing your face. And I've lived very happily, thank you. Why would I need even an ounce of friendship from you, let alone a romantic relationship?" She throws her hands up. "We don't have to do this. We live in the same city, but it's a big one. We don't need to ever see each other."

"Demi, I'm not an idiot. And neither are you. We're two grown people who can admit that the minute you stepped into that conference room, a spark was reignited. We'll never be friends, no, we never were. But I'm mature enough to admit that I feel an attraction towards you, and I know you feel one towards me. We have a past, yes, but we can rewrite it. I'm a different person, I'm not the asshole I was back then. And you can admit that each time you look at me, you know we could be something, too."

I hoped she'd lean in, give me at least just a little something. I wasn't crazy to think that we could pick up the tattered pieces of our college days and try to make something new work. Stitch a new quilt of those memories into something that lasted.

"I'm not sure what you want me to say, Paxton. Every time I look at you, I see how weak I was. I see how much you hurt me. How am I ever going to let go of that?"

I see the pain in her eyes, and I hate that I put it there.

"All I can tell you is that I am a different person. That the way you described what happens when people die ... I took that to heart. In the time we've been apart, I lost both of my parents. Tragically. And it changed every fiber within me. So that prick who hurt you? He's not here anymore. I know I can say that until the cows come home, but I'll prove it to you too."

Demi's face reflects the sympathy she feels for me, and I want to erase it.

"No, don't do that. Don't feel bad for me, and don't think I'm playing the orphan card to gain your trust. I'm simply saying that I lost the two people on this earth who loved me most, and it showed me how important love is. And right now, the only woman who I want to get to know more, who I could possibly love, is you. I'm not playing around. It's like I saw you and a switch flipped."

The doubt still lingered in her expression. "I don't know ..."

"You don't have to know." I was desperate now, and I could feel it to my marrow. "Just let me show you."

Exasperated, I see her relent. "If I let you show me, can I get in my car and drive home to take care of my dog?"

"Yes." I immediately move out of her way, because she gave me an inch and I don't want to take a mile.

Demi rolls her eyes again before she backs out of the parking spot and drives away.

I just smile to myself, knowing that I just did the single most important thing I've managed to do in a long time.

"I guess this makes lucky number seven. Are you going to forgive him?" My UPS delivery man, Chuck, brings hands the bouquet over.

My house is full of roses in every single color. White, red, pink ... you name the rose, Paxton Shaw has probably already bought it.

I smirk. "It is pretty hard to give someone a death glare when your house smells so darn good."

Chuck tips his hat. "Well, whatever the poor guy did, I think he's sorry about it."

He walks off after giving Maya a dog treat, and she happily runs into the living room to gobble crumbs off the carpet.

Since Monday morning, I've gotten seven humongous bouquets delivered to my front door. When Paxton had cornered me in the parking lot, I hadn't really believed he'd show me why I should give him another chance.

But if there was any way to a woman's heart, especially one who liked to garden, it was a beautiful flower arrangement. Or seven of them.

He'd looked so contrite a week ago, standing in front of me

talking about his parents. I knew what it was like to lose a loved one, how it changed the very fabric of your being. So when I looked at him, I saw the complete destruction he caused to my heart.

But maybe, just maybe, I could believe that an event so tragic had altered the way he viewed the world, and how it made him treat people now.

I still had so many reservations, so why did I smile every time I walked past my kitchen counter full of flowers? And why did I keep picturing his face, those full lips, as he talked about us and what we could be?

The ache in the middle of my chest that I thought I'd put out so long ago had resurfaced, pulling at me and making my finger-tips tingle when I thought about Pax. Did I want to admit that he was right? That the reason I hadn't settled down, had broken off my engagement, was because I still had feelings for him. That he was the earth and I was the moon, and I couldn't help but get pulled back to him.

Of course I still had feelings for him, that much was obvious. I couldn't go three seconds these days without daydreaming about how much he turned me on when we were in college, and how much he'd matured since then. He was like a Hemsworth brother, only sexier, if that was possible. I had to clench my thighs each time I thought about the dusting of stubble that painted his strong jaw. My nipples hardened every time I thought about how he'd used those cherry-crushed lips on me before, and how long it had been since any man had used any set of lips anywhere on me.

Maya barks next to me and I jump, not noticing she had come into the sun-filled kitchen. Caught daydreaming about sex red-handed.

"Hi pretty girl, did you finish your bone?" I bend down, rubbing my cheek on her snout.

She sits in front of me, her earnest brown eyes staring deeply into mine. Sometimes, I thought she could actually sense what was weighing on my mind.

Maya licked my cheek, giving me a slobbery wet kiss.

"Thank you for the kiss, lovely." I kiss her snout too.

We nuzzle for a minute more, before she pulls back to look at me.

"Should I give him another chance? Does he pass your test?" I mutter, more thinking out loud than actually asking my dog a question she'll never be able to answer.

Not that she physically answers any question.

Maya barks again, almost smiling at me as she does a circle, signaling that she wants to play.

"Okay, fine, let's go outside, you goof. All of these flowers are going to my head anyway."

Except I still smile one more time as I pass them before opening the door to my backyard and throwing the ball for my girl.

I probably shouldn't have lured her here under false pretenses, but Ryan had said he wanted to help and I couldn't deny a sick kid his right to watch true love blossom. Right?

"What did you tell her, again?" I bounced up and down, too much adrenaline rushing through my veins.

I was a grown man. I didn't get nervous. Not in front of thousands of people, and not in crucial games that had every thing riding on them.

But when it came to Demi these days, I was a sweating ball of stress.

"I told her that there was a charity flag football game I was competing in, and I wanted her to come." His toothy smile makes me laugh, and I fist bump him for being a sneaky little genius.

"I mean, it's not a total lie. You are playing a flag football game. It just isn't for charity and we won't be joining you. Although, I love hanging out with you buddy."

Ryan tosses me the football, glancing over his shoulder at where the game is happening. A couple dozen kids from his throw around, getting their flag belts all hooked on. It makes me happy that even though he's going through one of the toughest things anyone could ever imagine, especially at that age, that he still feels good enough to come out and play. He's one hell of a special person.

"As long as you send me the jersey we were talking about. And tickets to the playoff game." Ryan does a little dance and I laugh.

"You drive a hard bargain, but you know I'd happily do it even if you weren't being a great wingman right now."

Just then, Ryan runs forward a little, his skinny legs doing a jitterbug. I look across the park, which is packed on an exceptionally nice Saturday, and there she is.

Out of all of the hundreds of humans gallivanting in the grass right now, my eyes can't see a thing but her. Demi has always been the prettiest girl in the room, and her beauty has only increased in the time I've been away from her.

She walks towards Ryan, waving and happy, until she sees me standing just a few feet over from him. Then her expression turns to a scowl, and she shakes her head at me.

"Really? You used the kid?" Demi bends down to hug Ryan, but speaks to me, her brown eyes all disapproval.

I hold up my hands, innocent. "Hey, it was his idea."

Ryan releases her. "It was, technically. Now, I gotta go. Have a romantic lunch." He winks at her. "Give him a chance, he L-O-V-E-S you."

We both laugh at his spelling of the word, and I run a hand through my hair as she blushes.

A few beats go by before I speak. "Well, this isn't awkward."

Demi is standing in front of me, and I can see she is unsure if she should stay. "Well, you got me here."

"Yes, and thank you for coming. And staying, when you saw that it was in fact the asshole trying to woo you and not the cute kid who you adore." I motion to the spread on the ground. "I've made us a picnic. A lunch time, no expectations, no pressure, picnic."

Demi's mouth curves into a small smile. "Okay, Casanova. I'll stay. But only as long as I can eat all the prosciutto."

She eyes the cheese plate I've put on the checkered blanket, and I can practically see her mouth water.

What the hell would my brother, or my teammates, say about me planning a romantic picnic? They'd call me whipped, is what they'd say. They should have seen me researching how to pack a picnic basket, and looking up the best charcuterie ingredients. I thought my dick was going to just about fall off. But I was too concerned with picking the perfect finger sandwiches and stemless wine glasses to care.

It was a good thing I'd spent my money on basically nothing and no one in eight years, because I'd bought the best of everything for my one shot at convincing Demi to give this a real chance. I'd even flown in some fancy wine from Italy that one of the defensive linemen, Jared Jones, had recommended.

"Did you get home in time for your dog the other night?" I sit down, pouring out glasses and unpacking more food out of the basket.

In the distance, parents cheer for the children playing in Ryan's game and we glance over.

Demi's eyes trace back to me slowly, and she picks up the glass I set down in front of her. "I did, although she took twenty minutes to go to the bathroom and I could have strangled her. But at the same time, she is the most adorable thing since sliced bread, so ..."

I chuckle. "Didn't realize sliced bread was adorable."

She rolls her eyes. "You know what I mean."

"How old is she?" I set out the food, and take a risk by making her a plate.

I must have picked correctly, because she doesn't make a snarky comment or roll her eyes, just simply starts nibbling at the spread I've given her. Inside, I pump my fist and pretend to put one mark on the board in my favor.

It's clear that Demi loves her dog, by the way her eyes light up and small smile touches her full lips. "Maya is three, a golden retriever who loves grilled cheese sandwiches and watching rain storms through my sliding glass door."

"Wow, sounds like my perfect match on a dating website. Is she single?" I pop an olive in my mouth and realize how hungry I am.

I was so nervous, that I think I forgot to eat breakfast this morning. And maybe dinner last night. Which for an athlete, is unheard of. I usually consume about five thousand calories a day, and that is a strictly tailored diet of protein, carbs and healthy greens. I'm straying from that during this picnic, but the food was expensive and tastes delicious. And I'd been good my entire career, always following everything to the letter to improve my performance. Now that I was near the end, I could feel myself slipping.

Not just in my diet and exercise habits, but in my personal life as well. I could feel my slide into normalcy, descending from the mountain of champions and stardom to a mortal who would go on dates, mow the lawn, learn how to make pancakes for my kids on a Sunday morning. I couldn't wait for those things. As much as it was bittersweet that this would be my last season, a fact I hadn't told many people or announced in the media, I was ready in a way. Ready to become a normal guy, living in the suburbs, letting something bigger than sports or fame dictate and consume me. Letting love, hopefully, consume me.

"She lays down with dogs, but even you are too big of a dog for her." Demi smiles, and I know that she's only half-joking. "So, do you like being back in Charlotte?"

The first question she's asked me that isn't laced with malice or that rhetorical quality as if she doesn't really care about the answer.

I look at her, really look at her. And again, I want to mentally kick myself in the balls. Not realistically, because that fucking hurts, but I'm such a moron for treating this girl the way I did all those years ago.

Clearing my throat, because I realize Demi is looking at me like I have three heads, I stop staring so hard and answer her. "It's a blast from the past, in more ways than one. I'll find myself walking down a street, or driving through a certain neighborhood, and remember peeing behind a bush I see on the side of the road. I did a lot of dumb, drunk things here in my youth. So I guess it's fun to remember, but also strange for this old man."

"Old man? You're thirty, Pax."

Her nickname on my lips makes my stomach dip. "In the league, that is ancient. I guess playing football, you always think of yourself as older than you actually are. These young hotshots come in there, their balls barely dropped and walking around like they own the fucking planet. Meanwhile, I'm icing my back after every tackle and taking multivitamins. You should see my pill container, it's like I'm in a nursing home."

That makes her laugh, the sound akin to angels flying, or puppies barking, or something equally as cute. "Well, I think that old dogs are wiser, and can be more handsome."

Tilting my head, I move in a little closer. "Demi Rosen, are you flirting with me?"

She doesn't pull away, those long eyelashes fluttering in a slow blink. "I must have forgotten to take *my* meds this morning."

"Must have." I murmur, stroking a finger along her cheek.

Demi doesn't run, but I see the fear. I have to do this right, erase all the memories of me being a dirtbag from her brain. I know she has regret and hurt tattooed on her heart, and I put it there. So I can't take anything that she hasn't explicitly given me. I can't push her whatsoever, I have to let her call the shots this time around.

Her teeth sink into her bottom lip, and I know it's a reflex ... something she can't control. I've seen her do it a hundred times before, in my bed, in a closet at a party, in the shadowed tree line just out of sight.

The sound of afternoon sports games ring out in the park, music and chatter and birds filling up any leftover air space.

I lean further in, and can hear how shallow both hers and my breathing is. "I want to kiss you right now. Believe me, there is nothing I want more. But I'm not going to. When I kiss you for the first time, in a long time, I want you to give me permission. I want you to be completely sure, to make the call. So, Demi, can I kiss you?"

We're in a trance, a bubble of our own surrounded by hundreds of people all going about their own business.

"No." The word is a breath, a whisper, but her eyes say yes.

Immediately, I take my hand away from her jaw. "What you say goes. I promise."

We can't stop looking at each other, and even though that animalistic need to capture her mouth rages inside me, I won't pursue it.

Not until she tells me I can.

16

DEMI

I t's funny; parts of this feel so familiar, and parts of it feel so new that it's throwing me for a loop.

After the picnic lunch, and the almost kiss, Paxton packs all of the empty containers and blanket into the backpack he's brought and throws it on his back.

"Let's go for a walk." He lifts his big, lean body, offering me a hand once he's standing.

Is it bad that my stomach flutters when he pulls me up, his muscled arm acting as if I weigh about two pounds? It reminds of the time we had sex, him holding me up against the wall and impaling—

"You okay?" Pax looks at me, his eyes happy and bright.

I can't help but blush. Do you think he knows what I was just thinking about? "Yep, I'm fine."

My voice is a bit high, but we start to walk. There is an unsettled tension between us since I told him he couldn't kiss me, but he seems to have taken it with a grain of salt and moved right past it. Just like that, he'd pulled back and kept his hands to himself, a pure gentleman move. I wasn't used to it, not from Paxton Shaw.

I also wasn't used to him wanting to kiss me in broad daylight, in front of people. I was trained to expect stolen glances, midnight texts, anything but sweetness and asking for permission. This reserved, polite man is a new version of a person I used to hate ... so could I hate him still?

I was so conflicted that I almost miss Paxton stopping mid-stride and asking me a question.

"Want some?" Pax points to an Italian ice vendor, and I nod, always in the mood for a sweet treat.

We walk over together, wait in line behind a cute family with their infant daughter, the cherry ice dribbling down her chin as her mom tries to feed it to her.

"I'll take a blueberry please, and the lady will have ...?" Pax pauses, his wallet open as he waits for my answer.

"I'll have cherry, thanks."

We get our water ice and keep walking, the sweetness cooling me down after sweat pooled in my bra at having this man almost kiss me.

Pax looks over at me, about to say something, when a silly smile breaks out on his mouth. "You have ..."

He points at my chin, and I self-consciously swipe at it. "What? Did I get some on me?"

Laughing, he keeps pointing. "You didn't get it."

"Get it!" I giggle, not wanting it to drip onto my shirt.

Pax reaches out, his thumb expertly wiping my skin. Pinpricks of lust tingle down my spine, and I bite back a sigh. "See, this is another instance where I would kiss you if I had your permission."

I smile, this situation significantly less laden with sexual tension than when we were on the blanket. "You just really want to kiss me, huh?"

"*Yes*," he answers immediately.

I have to laugh. "How do you even know it will be any good?"

Pax cocks an eyebrow. "I think we've had enough practice for me to know that it would be pretty spectacular."

I concede, his hand pulling away once more. I miss the heat of his fingers. "Okay, fine, I think you have me there."

"Now stop taunting me and eat your Italian ice," he huffs, jokingly.

"Stop being a horndog," I counter.

"So, since I've seen you, tell me, what has been the most exciting adventure you've been on?" He completely changes the subject.

"Slick, trying to move away from the awkward sexual pink elephant in the room." I tip my head to him, as if there were a hat on it. "But I'll bite. I went to Israel with my parents last year for Rosh Hashanah. It was incredible. I mean, I've been before, it's my favorite place on earth, but going during the high holy days was ... I don't even have words for it."

He seems genuinely interested in what I'm saying. "I've never been, but I've heard it's awesome. I'd love to float in the Dead Sea. Or is that a tourist trap?"

I chuckle. "I mean, it is a tourist trap, but it's a totally cool tourist trap. The mud makes your skin feel amazing afterward, and you literally cannot sit up in the water. It's hard to put your feet on the sea floor, that's how buoyant the human body is in that water. You feel ... weightless. Some people think it's hokey, but I found it ... freeing. When I went, I walked miles down the beach, to a spot where almost no one was, and floated for about an hour."

We sit on a bench, our treats all but gone. "That sounds very relaxing."

"Better than any spa treatment I've ever had. But it's not just that, Israelis have this outlook on life that is just so different from ours. Meals last hours, sometimes days. They're jovial and celebratory, but fiercely serious on sacred days. It's just ... a different world. And one that I love to be a part of as often as I can be."

Pax nods, and I find myself wanting to know what he's been up to. "How about you? Lots of Vegas trips and flashy nightclubs?"

He frowns, more at himself than me. "Nope. My best adventure, if you can even call it that, was two years ago when my brother and I rented a house on Lake Michigan for three weeks in the off-season. We just fished and had bonfires in the backyard, listened to country music, drank beers. It was a total dude-fest in the middle of nowhere, and it was the best time of my life."

I was surprised. I thought he would have said Monaco or Cancun. But instead, he'd detailed a bonding trip with his brother that sounded as modest as a church mouse.

"That sounds great, very relaxing ... but a lot less low-key than I remember you being."

He nods, the sun going down in the sky as the time passes. "Well, you have a lot to relearn about me. I liked that trip because I was with family, and it was just simple. No press, no expectations, no fancy suits or need to be *on*. Now that retirement is on the horizon, that's what I'm looking forward to the most."

"Retirement? You're so young." I was confused.

Paxton smiles. "I find it refreshing that you still know nothing about sports. Anyways, I'm yesterday's news. A geezer in the eyes of the league. And I'm not going to be one of those athletes who keeps chugging along, even though he and the whole world knows he's washed up. So, this is my last year. But don't tell the press, they'll be all over me like white on rice."

I pretend to lock my lips and throw away the key. "I won't say a thing. Or let anyone know how many corny metaphors you use."

Pax rolls his eyes, but those full lips tip up.

"So, this is it, huh? And what's next? It's not like you ever need to work again. And I'm not saying that to find out how much you make, I know it's enough that you can afford to donate half a million dollars to Ryan's chemo unit at the children's hospital."

Yeah, I knew about his donation. Ryan's mother had called me to thank me for introducing Pax into their lives, and she'd told me what he'd done for the hospital that her son had his treatment at. He'd made it without a peep to my company, or the media, or anyone else. That was true giving, and it was one of the reasons why I was giving him a second chance.

He ignores my comment, choosing not to even brag a little about his donation. "I don't know what I'm going to do. For so long, my life has been go, go, go. The next workout, the next game, the next season. I've starved myself, binged on protein, worked my muscles to the brink, done interviews until my cheeks hurt from fake smiling. I think, honestly, I'm just going to be happy to have some solitary time to myself."

I nod, because I understood that. "Alone time is some of my favorite time. I hope you can find that after this season is over."

"Well, I didn't say I wanted to be completely alone." In a risky move, and without asking, Pax laces his fingers through mine as we walk back toward the parking lot bordering the park.

"I thought you were going to ask my permission." I don't pull my hand away though.

He shrugs, his fingers in mine feeling like the best thing in the world at this moment. "If I didn't push you a bit, I'd be stuck in the friend zone for the next however many years and this old geezer doesn't have that kind of time."

I rolled my eyes for the thousandth time on this date, but shifted my hand so that it nestled closer to his. And I didn't let go until he opened my car door and told me good night.

Nine Years Ago

The pins crashing against the hardwood of the lane rang out through the entire bowling alley, and Jamison patted himself on the back as he walked back to our table.

"Take that, motherfuckers." His big body, that of an outside linebacker, squeezed into the booth.

A few of the girls squealed, and two empty beer bottles tipped over. The end of the lane was littered with people, shoes, and drinks, making it difficult to move. We occupied almost half of Bowl-O-Rama, the football team having had the great idea to take over the local spot because we were bored with the downtown bars on the weekend. And we were all competitive as hell, so there was that.

With us came other guys friends, groupies, actual girlfriends, and other groups of college students who had heard we were taking over and just wanted to be a part of something.

I sat in the middle of it all, Demi under my arm, ruling roost amongst my teammates. "You piece of shit, you're not going to beat me."

I sent a cocky smile across the sticky booth we were all crowded in, and a couple of the guys raised a beer to me.

"Your team ain't shit, Shaw." He rumbled, slamming a shot back.

Looking up at the scoreboard overhead, we were down by only ten points in the last frame. And Demi was up.

"Go get em, baby." I kissed her on the cheek, and she stood, myself and a couple other pairs of eyes staring at her ass.

Fuck, she was hot. We had been hooking up for a long time on and off, but lately, we'd been more on than any other time. So on, in fact, that I'd driven her here tonight and had spent most of the night trying to stick my hands down the waistband of her jeans.

She seemed a little bit shocked, and maybe uncomfortable, by all the public displays of affection. But, what could I say? Football season was over, we'd won a championship, and I had drank about five beers. I was happy, and horny, and she was a good lay. And she wasn't bad to talk to, as far as indulging in conversation with women went.

Demi picked up the ball she'd been using, the look of concentration on her face kind of cute. She wasn't half bad at bowling, and I was glad I'd picked her to bring tonight instead of some other girl. When she'd given me an ultimatum a few months back, to either be with her exclusively or never talk to her again, I'd given in. We hadn't tried it yet, and while I wasn't looking for a girlfriend at all, I could do the whole monogamy without a title thing for a little. Or, at least, I could try.

It had its perks, mainly the consistent, mind-blowing sex, but I had my whole life to settle down. And for a guy like me, I had my pick of girls like I had number of flavors available in an ice cream shop. Endless possibilities.

"Dude, your girlfriend is fine. Like, if you want to Eiffel Tower, I'd be down." Our wide receiver, Nathan, sits down next to me.

"One, she's not my girlfriend." I chug the rest of my beer. "Two, I don't share. You wanna see another guy's dick in the bedroom, ask Jamison."

Jamison chuckles. "Man, you're missing out. Tag-teaming is *fucking fun*."

Demi turns around, waving slightly before lining up to bowl. She has no idea what we're talking about, and her cheeks would probably turn bright red if she did. That's another thing I liked about her, that sweet innocence that was still so prominent even after how I'd tarnished her.

"And if she isn't your girlfriend, you don't mind if we take a ride." Nathan was goading me, just like the rest of the guys on the team.

It was an unspoken rule that Demi was mine, but I'd never explicitly staked claim. I didn't want to date her, but I sure wanted to fuck her. And what I wanted, I got without questions. Keep your star player happy.

But since we'd gone exclusive, at least when it came to me not sticking my cock in other girls, the guys had a bet going of when I'd actually introduce her as my girlfriend.

I was in on the bet, a hundred bucks put on the outcome that I'd never actually put a title on it.

"Don't get cocky, Nathan. Plus, a girl like Demi would never go for you in a million years." I smiled at him.

"Yeah, not when she sucks homeboy's dick whenever he snaps his fingers." Jamison snickers.

A pang of grief moves through me, because I'm being an asshole talking like this about the girl who really does like me when she's only a few feet away, but I have to keep up appearances. I'm Big Bad Paxton Shaw.

Demi bowls, the ball curving a bit but straightening out halfway down the lane. It rolls and rolls, finally hitting the pins and knocking them all down.

She whirls around with a high-pitched squeal, throwing her hands up in the air so that her crop top rides up even farther. Bouncing over to me, I stand to catch her.

"We won!" She cries out as she jumps into me, and I catch her in one strong arm.

"You did it, that's my girl." I whisper, a growl vibrating into her ear.

She shivers, and I know I have her. I know I can ask her to do anything in this moment, and she'll do it no questions asked.

18

"I want to see the new case files."

My heels clack along the tile floors of our office, my staff in various stages of work. Justin is on the phone, arranging flights for one of our families. Gina was arranging marketing material and coordinating some press for a couple of events we would be attending.

And I was trying to fulfill the wishes of every child who applied to our nonprofit. I made it back to my desk, after one of my employees handed me four files, and laid them out in front of me. One was a little girl with Lupus, who wanted to travel to the American Girl Store in New York City. Another boy, a teenager with stage three leukemia, wished to go backstage at a Walk the Moon concert. And so on. The wishes never stopped, and neither did these terrible illnesses that I wished I could stop.

I wish there was more time, for them. But if there couldn't be, I would create more time for myself. To grant each dream, to give them some sort of semblance of normalcy.

By the time I looked up, it was an hour and a half later. And lunchtime, which I often skipped.

As if reading my mind, Farrah walked in with takeout bags. "You know, if you don't eat, you'll just be useless at your job."

I wipe a hand across my brow, my stomach grumbling. "That's not true. One day I just drank about three pots of coffee, and I arranged for seven wishes."

"I think that's called being cracked out. Please, take a few minutes and eat." She doesn't give me a choice, just starts laying sushi containers out on top of the files on my desk.

"So, you haven't wanted to go to the bar lately, huh?"

Her voice has an edge of already knowing something, and I feel like I'm walking into a trap.

It's been two weeks since Paxton's misleading setup in the park, and since then I haven't been out to a happy hour with Farrah. Instead, the man who hadn't ever called me back in college, was calling and texting me almost every second of the day. It was like he was overcompensating for all the times he'd done me wrong ... and I couldn't say that I didn't enjoy it.

"I just haven't felt up to going out recently," I lie through my teeth.

No one knows about Paxton yet, not that we were together in college and not that we're ... dating, I guess, now. Technically, it's only been two dates. One in the park and another dinner last week. He'd walked me to my car, I'd insisted on driving separately, and he hadn't kissed me. It was both maddening and cute that he wanted me to approve it.

"Try again." She shoves a piece of spicy tuna roll in her mouth.

"Excuse me?" I start to sweat.

Farrah shoots me a look like I've been caught red handed. "You're blushing more. You look at your phone every ten seconds during the day. And I haven't heard one of your 'I'm better off alone' speeches in a while. You're dating someone, I just know it."

But did she know who? It didn't seem like it, so I pondered how to answer. I kind of wanted to talk to someone about it, and since I couldn't call Chels because she would slaughter me, Farrah was my next best choice.

"You caught me." I held my chopsticks up.

She laughed and pointed her finger at me. "I knew it! You're so getting laid!"

I looked down, shaking my head. "Actually, I'm so not."

Farrah gives me a pointed look, her eyes slanting. "Please explain."

Sighing, I fill her in without telling her it's Paxton. "I'm seeing this guy that ... I have a past with. It's super complicated, and I mean with a capital *C*. It's like when you knot your favorite necklace into a thousand tangles and know you want to wear it, but can't seem to figure out how."

Farrah nods. "I fucking hate when that happens."

"Yeah, well, that's what is happening. And I like him, really like him ... but, I feel like it's too good to be true."

Her face lights up and her mouth forms a big *O*. "Since I've known you, since I've been working here from the day you hired me five years ago, you've only had history with one guy. Are you dating Zachary?!"

I chuckle, because if only she knew how much I wished I could be completely happy dating my ex-fiancé. "No, it's not him."

Her face grows solemn. "So this is him, then?"

Panic seizes me, because maybe she does know that I'm seeing Pax. "Who?"

"The guy who fucked you up so royally that you're no longer a whole person."

It was blunt, so hard in its delivery that it was like a gunshot to my heart. Was I that broken, that deeply broken, that it showed in my every day interactions?

"How ...?" I was so shocked she'd said that, that I almost couldn't form words.

She sighed, setting down the piece of sushi she was about to eat. That was Farrah though, bluntly honest to form, so matter of fact that sometimes it was icy.

"Demi, besides Zachary, which I could see was doomed from the start, you've never dated one guy in the five years I've known you. I never said anything, because I wouldn't want to be bothered about my past or love life and so I don't do it to others, but you were fucking damaged. You couldn't talk to a guy without a frown on your face by the end, and your trust issues extend into friendships as well. Did you know it took almost two years for you to actually accept an invite to drinks with me?"

I hadn't, and that was sad. "I need to do this."

Resuming her eating, she stuffed a roll in her mouth. "I know you do. If it allows you closure, I'm all for it. If you fall in love, if this is really your one, then you fucking deserve it. Like I said, I've never felt your aura be this happy."

I choked on a piece of salmon at her use of such a homeopathic kind of diagnosis. "I wasn't aware you could read auras."

She nodded vigorously. "Oh yes, and yours is deep orange right now. That relates to the reproductive organs and emotions ... means you're having vigorous energy and creativity now with a dash of adventure and courage."

I stare at her, dumbfounded. "I'm not even going to ask where you learned that."

"Good idea. Now, would you stop bragging about your love life and let me get back to work." Farrah rolls her eyes like she didn't just ambush my office and force me to open up.

I laugh, throwing a file across my desk. "Let's try to make this wish happen."

One of the most important things I'd learned from my time in the league, and just from playing football in general, was to go after everything you wanted with a vigor that would not take no for an answer.

In every contract negotiation, I went in with a clear head and my terms, exactly how I wanted them. I'd never been turned down or given less than what I'd asked for.

During every play, I went my hardest and ran smart routes, choosing my spots and succeeding in bringing victory to my team.

And with Demi, I wasn't about to back down just because I had built some tough ass obstacles for myself to overcome.

This time, she had actually agreed to go out with me. Instead of me having to force her there using a child and a his illness. Sure, I could tell she was still skeptical, but I was wearing her down, and that was a tactic I knew how to use well. I'd gotten my ass beaten by huge defensive linemen for years, and I could tell you, Demi Rosen was probably tougher than all of them combined.

No, not probably. Definitely.

Setting the knotted rope I'd just secured down, I put a hand over my eyes to watch the dock for visitors. I'd told her to meet me here, knowing she would want to drive herself so she'd have an escape if she wanted it.

However, I'd outsmarted her on this one. Getting her on a boat, where she had no escape, would force her to open up a little more to me. Unless she really wanted to escape me, in which case she could abandon ship and swim back to the dock at Tailrace Marina. I wouldn't put that past her.

Since moving back to Charlotte, I'd had one of my boats transported to the marina just outside the city. I know, it sounds obnoxious saying just *one* of my boats, but I was a boy who'd grown up on them. My salary afforded me the luxury of keeping up the hobby, and it was one of my only vices these days.

It was surprising to many that my parent's deaths hadn't stunted my love of the water. But if anything, I felt more connected to them when I was out there, free from the land and cutting through the depths of oceans or lakes. Out there, on the open water, you answered to no one. You could just ... be. And I was free to feel anyway I wanted about my parents. Happy, for their love of the water and the way they taught us to love it. Sad, that it had taken them way too early. Scared, that I would never find the kind of love that I hadn't realized they'd given me until it was too late.

"He's athletic, charitable, a celebrity, knows how to sail boats ... seriously, is there anything you aren't good at?" Demi stands at the beginning of the gangway that leads up to my boat, her hands on her hips.

She looks like some picture out of a sailboat magazine, one of those slender, elegant models posing in Monte Carlo or something. Her outfit is lightyears more sophisticated than my cargo shorts and T-shirt. She probably went out and bought the perfect sailing attire, just for this occasion. It was cute, and I knew she cared about this.

"Math, fucking terrible at it. Hence why I chase a ball around a field instead of trade commodities." I joke, wiping my hands off and going to help her up the gangway.

I take her hand, leading her up onto the deck, and take the oversized bag she has slung over her shoulder. When I pick it up, I almost drop it, not expecting it to be that heavy.

"Holy shit, what the hell is in here?"

"A woman never reveals her secrets." She winks at me.

"Yeah, because she carries them all in her ginormous bag. Why do women do that? Why do they need a bag the size of Texas? You can't possibly need half the stuff in here." We walk to the cushioned benches, and she sits, removing her sandals.

"I need all of it. What if I get a blister on my heel? I have BandAids and Neosporin. Happen to get hungry? I've got snacks. Need to follow up on emails? My tablet is charged and ready. Haven't you ever wondered how women can multitask like men never could? It's partially the bag."

I chuckle, because Demi is so damn sexy explaining things to me while practically undressing. She's shed her sandals and the light sweater she had on, leaving her in a one-piece bathing suit that's making my mouth water, and white linen pants. The sun catches her hair, the strands of light brown glistening. I want to kiss her, capture her mouth and make her succumb to me, but I hold back. My nails dig into my palms as I force my cock to quiet down.

"Whatever you say. Now, why don't you go sit up there while I cast us off?" I point to the cushions on the back of the boat, the ones that give the best view of the retreating harbor.

She smiles, a raw, happy expression, and quickly bounces over to them. I want to give her some time to herself, after all, I think this is probably a rare moment for her. From what I can gather from the team, and from Demi on the couple of dates we've been on now, she is a total workaholic. Today is the first time she's agreed to take a break for me, and I want her to feel comfortable and relaxed before I really turn the charm on. I'm determined to open her up, and maybe get the kiss I've been waiting for.

We spend the first half an hour of the date apart; me working hard to adjust and steer and get us into the water smoothly. It's hard work, one that leaves my muscles burning and the eye for detail sharp.

Demi lays back on the sundeck, watching the big sails go up, and letting the sun wash over her face. When I finally lower the anchor, securing our position in the open sea, I make my way to her with beers in hand.

"You know, I typically don't drink beer." She examines it before clinking her bottle against mine and taking a sip.

"What, you got too sophisticated since your days of drinking Keystone out of kegs?" I nestle closer to her.

Our knees are touching as we lounge next to each other, and being this close to her without touching her face or pulling her waist into mine is killing me.

She lightly taps my shoulder in a playful hit. "College doesn't count. You'll drink anything that's cheap and/or free."

"True." I let the silence settle over us, the water lapping at the boat.

"You love it out here, don't you?" Her brown eyes examine me.

"I do." I nod, not needing to explain further.

"It reminds you of them." It's not a question from her, just a statement.

I forget that she knows me. And she also knows people dealing with death and grieving. And it's her job to know how to make it better. In some ways, even after all of these years since losing my parents, that is a comfort.

We finish our beers, not needing to fill the air with chatter. Maybe this is what it's like to find the person who most truly fits you. The kind of relationship that doesn't need words or banter, although those are nice. The ability to sit in comfortable, companionable silence ... perhaps that's how you know you've found her.

After another gap of time, I reach over, lacing my fingers through Demi's. Our eyes meet, and every emotion within her is communicated to me. She's letting me see her fear, her lust, her willingness, her hope.

"You can kiss me now." The words are quiet, but there is no wavering in her tone.

I cup her cheek, pausing just centimeters from her lips to look more deeply into her eyes. And then we both flutter our lids closed, and I lean in.

The kiss is soft, searching. A coming home after years apart. The taste of her, the exploration of our lips and tongues together, makes me dizzy. Stokes the fire inside me, sending both lust and the sensation of falling in love spiraling down my spine.

I don't stop. I just keep kissing her, over and over now that I'm allowed. Hours pass, the sun starts to set, and still, I can't pry my mouth from hers.

This day should be endless. It should last and last until nothing else fills me but Demi.

M others are known to bring all sorts of guilt, at least that's what they say.

Guilt about not calling them enough, not coming by for lunch, not doing what they thought would be the best thing to do, in any situation.

But if you don't have a Jewish mother, you know absolutely nothing about guilt.

"Sweetheart, it looks like you decided to get the challah from that new bakery." My mother, Sarah, stands in my kitchen, scrutinizing each thing I've made for Friday night Shabbat dinner.

What she doesn't say is that she would have bought the challah she'd used for my entire life, from the bakery she frequented near her house, but that I couldn't find at the grocery store. This would be a point of contention for years now, she'd bring it up every time we had challah. The time I bought the wrong kind. Thankfully, I got the right gefilte fish.

"It's challah, Mom. It's on the side and we dip it in soup or spread butter or gefilte fish on it. It all tastes the same." I roll my eyes but smile because I love having my parents around.

Jews from Queens, they had that East Coast attitude through

and through. They'd grown up with money, but both sets of my grandparents had made them work from the age of fifteen. They'd made something of themselves, a professor of literature and an accountant respectively. Mom had stocked my library with the classics, while Dad had always taught me the importance of finance and numbers. Even now, my father went through my books with me each quarter to make sure the business, it's taxes, and reports were properly filed.

When I'd moved down to Charlotte, my parents had said goodbye to the cold weather and followed me. Now my father freelanced, my mother was retired but spent her time volunteering at the local library, and we had dinner almost every Friday night.

"It's a good-looking brisket, *bubbala*." My dad, Aaron, slices the meat and places it on the white platter I placed out specifically for it.

It was my week to host, and while I was dead tired, conversation and time spent with my parents could never be beat.

"Thanks, Dad. The soup is almost done, and we have to wait for one more person, and then we'll be ready."

I went to the cabinet to grab the Manischewitz and avoided my mother's beady stare.

"One more?" Her tone is way too excited.

If my mother could have sold me off and had ten grandchildren by the time I was twenty-two, she would have.

"Yes, one more." I hustle into my dining room, getting away from her curious questions and proud looks.

I hadn't been sure if I wanted to introduce Paxton to my parents yet, but when I'd mentioned Shabbat dinner, his ears had perked up. He was just crazy enough to want an invite, and he'd worn me down until I reluctantly said he could join us.

Good thing for my sense of humor, he had absolutely no idea what he was in for.

"Who is this young man?" Mom practically jumps on me as I set the table.

Part of me wants to brag, but the child in me wants to withhold facts from my mother simply because it's kind of fun to watch her squirm.

"You're going to meet him in about twenty minutes, can't you just wait?"

She stops, clutching the gold Jewish star necklace that she always wears. "Demi Rachel Rosen. I have waited thirty whole years for this moment. You will not keep me in suspense one minute longer."

Like I said, buckets of guilt.

I give them the only piece of information that I know they'll grill Paxton about. "I will say this ... he's not Jewish."

My mother says, "Oy vey" at the same time my father pops his head in and demands, "What?"

"He is not Jewish. And don't act so enraged, you'd rather have me happy than unmarried." I knew this to be very true.

My parents look at me, their gazes unapproving but I also know they're seeing my reasoning.

"As long as he's a mensch, I'll give him a chance." My mother inclines her head, and my father doesn't say a word.

He learned long ago not to disagree with my mother. Even if she was wrong, explaining why she was took more effort than just staying silent.

Twenty minutes later, exactly on the dot, Paxton shows up with flowers in one hand and a bakery box in the other. He presents them to my mother, who wraps him in a big hug and I know instantly that he's sold her.

"Oh, look, *bubbala*, he brought rugelach!" She is so over the moon about him already, I can tell.

When she turns her back, Paxton mouths the nickname at

me and raises an eyebrow. Why do I know that he's going to tease me for that later?

Mom joins Dad in the dining room, and Pax uses the moment to steal a kiss. Now that I've given him the go ahead, he won't stop kissing me. And I'm not complaining, the man could win a Lombardi trophy for making out.

We all sit down for dinner, and Dad immediately starts in. "Wait a minute, you're that football player ..."

Pax chuckles, looking at me. "Now I see where you get your love of sports."

It's true, my family has never been big into organized athletic events. I'm not sure why, but my parents never gave a crap about this country's obsession with grown men chasing, hitting or catching balls.

"You play football? How nice!" My mom bats her eyelashes at him, and all criticism of him not being Jewish is seriously outside with Elijah.

"Either that or I run around a field trying to catch a ball like a five-year-old. My profession is basically for overgrown boys who never grew up."

"You've got chutzpah, kid. I'll give you that." Dad stands with his wine glass, reaching to get more, and slaps Paxton on the back, grinning.

I shook my head and dropped it into my hands. Only my father would tell the leading tight end in the NFL that he had chutzpah.

Truth was, my father could care less what the person I dated did, or how much money they made. As long as they treated me with respect, he was okay with it. He'd always made that clear, not that I'd brought many boys around my folks.

The rest of dinner goes swimmingly, with my parents hanging on every word that Pax says, and my mother giving everyone grief.

"*Eat more. Eat!*"

"*Demi, I wish you'd wear your hair back more, I love it like that.*"

"*Aaron, not too much red meat, you know what it does to your stomach.*"

The only one she didn't chide was the man who seemed to have stolen all of our hearts. When it's time to go, my mom wraps me in a big hug.

"I'm just verklempt, I'm so happy. Mazel tov, sweetheart," Mom whispers in my ear as she kisses me goodbye.

The thing is, I'm verklempt, too. It's been a long time since a man made me this nervous, or this hot for him.

Come to think of it, Paxton had been the *only* guy to ever make me feel this way.

"I like you, even if you are a shegetz." Dad shakes Pax's hand as my parents make their way out.

"I'll get you guys tickets to next week's game, so you can come see what football looks like." Pax smiles good-naturedly.

They finally go, and it's sadly quiet without their hemming and hawing.

"They're freaking awesome." He takes me in his arms, pressing his lips against my forehead. "Thank you for letting me be a part of a family again."

I just settle into him, loving the feel of his warmth and strength around me. I don't say it, but I wasn't *letting* him be a part of my family. He was becoming part of it, way too quickly for my heart to process.

Fear gripped me, and yet, I didn't want to let him go. I didn't want him to go home, I wanted him to stay here. Uncertainty surrounded me, and the walls I'd carefully used to guard my heart since him didn't know whether to fortify themselves, or fall.

21

I buckle the strap to my tan suede block heels, smoothing the fabric over so that it all runs one way before I stand up. Looking at myself in the floor length mirror in my bedroom, I check my stomach to see if I can actually see the butterflies fluttering around in there.

My velvet green strapless ball gown is practically glued to me, every body part snug in its place inside he material. I picked the signature color because it was the one I always looked best in, my mocha-colored hair always meshing well with the shade. My earrings were simple, small diamond studs, ones I'd bought myself as a birthday present last year.

I was ready. Wish Upon a Star threw an annual gala every year. And like every year, I gave a speech. And like every year, I was dreading it.

I knew as the CEO of my own company that public speaking was a must. I just really hated doing it. I was articulate, sure, but I typically let me work speak for itself. Alas, we needed funding from some of the biggest players in Charlotte, and this is how we kept the lights on and were able to make so many dreams come true. So for that, I'd swallow back the nervous bile threatening to work it's way out of my throat and just get on with it.

There was a second reason I was so nervous tonight as well. I'd agreed to let Paxton escort me as my date.

He'd caught wind of the gala through a few guys on the team and in the Cheetahs organization who attended every year. And naturally, bugged me until I said he could go as my date.

My doorbell sounded, and Maya the cuddly guard dog barked. I quickly made my way downstairs, grabbing my clutch off the bed.

"Maya, shush. It's your favorite person."

It was true. Pax had been over to my house, never for the night though, a couple of times now, and Maya had all but peed on him and made him her own. Things with us had been going well, hence my letting him come to the gala. My parents asked about him every week that I spoke to or saw them, and he continued to send flowers or little treats to my office or home.

All in all, I was getting used to the idea that I could be with him again. And so was my body.

Our kissing had evolved from long, soft explorations to heated romps on the couch or in the car, to hands wandering and pulling at the fabric of clothes. Every time he touched me, I shivered. But for some reason, just before we crossed the line into southern territory, I put a stop to things. I couldn't move to the next ... base, to put a sports metaphor on things.

"Hi, beautiful!" Pax leans down when I open the door, his face covered by Maya kisses as he stuck a bone out for her to grab and devour.

"You spoil her." I shake my head, laughing.

He stands, letting me have a good long look at the gorgeous God in a tux before me. "And hello, gorgeous."

Pax holds out one single red rose, and I blush. The gesture is very romantic, and I let my heart be swept up in the moment.

His emerald eyes rake over me, embers burning in them when his gaze falls over my cleavage and collarbone. Stepping into the house, he doesn't pause before running his big, callused hands down my bare arms and pressing his lips to said collarbone.

"You taste delicious. Let's just stay here."

A throaty laugh escapes my lips. "I'm throwing the event."

"Farrah can handle it." He moves to my shoulder.

"Uh uh, no. Down boy." I push him off.

"I'm not the dog here."

"Oh, but you are." I raise an eyebrow at him. "You look very handsome."

"A regular power couple, we are. Now let's go, you're going to make us late." He chides me sarcastically, and I roll my eyes.

Forty minutes later, we're on the step and repeat, posing for photos. The press in attendance all wait their turn to interview me, my answers gracious and thorough. I love my job, so I schmooze to keep my business functioning. It's a necessary evil.

Moving through the grand ballroom of The Chauncy, a beautiful event space in downtown Charlotte, I take in Gina's work. Besides marketing, she's always had the best eye for design. Tonight, she's outdone herself. The chandeliers glisten above the dance floor, gold and crystal glistening from every corner of the room. Enormous white flower arrangements mark the middle of every table, becoming a conversation piece and centerpiece. The plates are lined with thing gold, ornate detail, while the water goblets and wine glasses match. The entire gala has a sophisticated, ethereal feel, and it's easy to get swept away in it's romance.

"Would you care to dance?" Paxton's hand meets the small of my back, and I want to melt into him.

Trying to keep a cool head, it would not be professional if everyone saw you make out with your date in the middle of the party, I nod. "I wasn't aware you had moves."

"Sweetheart, being light on my feet is part of my job description." He moves me to the middle of the dance floor, his arms bracketing my body.

The twelve piece band is playing an instrumental Sinatra tune, and I stare into Pax's eyes as we sway to the rhythm. And then he gets fancy, doing some footwork as he sweeps me across the hardwood. I have to laugh, because he's being so charming and my heart won't stop beating against my ribcage.

"You're too good at this." I murmur.

"What's that?" His lips meet my ear.

"Making me fall." It's honest, and I'm scared to say it, but it's out there.

He moves his head back so that we're eye to eye, and the expression on his face is so serious. His mouth opens, and he's about to respond, when we're interrupted.

"Demi Rosen! I've been looking everywhere for you."

I turn, seeing Chuck Gaskill standing right next to us. We've reached the edge of the dance floor, and the song has ended, so I move out of Paxton's embrace and go to greet Chuck.

Offering my cheek, I introduce him as we air kiss. "This is Chuck Gaskill, owner of the biggest catering company in Charlotte. He donated all of the food tonight, and is always a great partner whenever we need a wish fulfilled."

"What she means is, I give her a lot of money. But I'm happy to do so." The jovial, chubby man laughs, his entire body coming to life with the sound.

Pax stuck his hand out, putting on that typical all-star smile. "Paxton Shaw, nice to meet you. I'm her boyfriend."

The word boyfriend left me dumb-struck, and I swear I had to check if my jaw was on the floor. We hadn't discussed a title, nor what we were to each other. So much for not pushing things on me, or moving too fast.

Paxton Shaw was like an adorable bulldozer. He ran you over to get his way, but he looked damn cute doing it.

"Paxton Shaw, the wide receiver? Well, Demi, I didn't know you were dating a superstar." Chuck winks at me.

"Neither did I." I murmured under my breath.

"What's that, babe?" Pax gives me a toothy grin, and I know he's being smug.

"Nothing. Chuck, are you enjoying yourself?" I lace my hand through Pax's, the movement seeming second nature.

I squeeze, trying to let him know that I don't really want to talk to people anymore. We've been here for hours, or so it seems, and I just want to give my speech and go home. I've never been overly social, I'm much happier hanging out at home in front of the fireplace with a glass of wine and a good book.

"There is drink, food and beautiful women. What is not to like? So, how long have you two been knocking boots?"

Chuck was never subtle, and could care less about offending people.

"Well, if you must know, Chuck … I don't kiss and tell. Ever. So I'm going to take this woman and get her up to the podium where she has a speech to give."

Paxton to the rescue.

"Thank you," I mutter as we make our way to the stage. "I don't mind him usually, but he can be a lot."

"I wasn't about to tell him that I wish I could knock boots with you right now." His eyes are pure carnal fire.

I have to take a deep breath, because how inappropriate would it be to get on stage while thinking about getting him naked.

"Promise we can get out of here immediately after I do this?"

"Absolutely."

I keep my promise, whisking her out of the gala as soon as the applause dies down with her spectacular speech.

"You really did something." I nod my head, looking at her in the dim car light. "I know you are, but you should be damn proud. You're superwoman. I'm in awe."

The way those people had held onto every word, the stories she told about the wishes she and her staff had granted this year ... Demi was amazing. Plain and simple.

"Thanks." She blushes, her hand resting on my leg as I steer us toward her condo.

I'd seen her eyes when I called myself her boyfriend. I flashed back to a time when I made a bet ... and so much grief ran through my system that it was a wonder I didn't drop dead on the spot from being such an asshole to her all those years ago. It was a miracle she was even still sitting here with me, allowing me to escort her to her own gala and not slapping me in the face when I claimed her like some kind of caveman in front of a donor.

"I'm sorry about the whole boyfriend thing back there. I

know that we haven't discussed it, and it was piggish of me to say it for the first time without consulting you."

Demi studies me, her beautiful head tilting to the side. "You know, there was a time when I would have given anything to hear you put a title on our relationship. And now here you are, apologizing for being hasty and checking to make sure it's okay with me that you did so. That's how I know you've changed, Pax. The guy you were in college would have never done that. Would have never admitted he was wrong."

I give her a small smile. "We all have room to be a good person when someone lets us."

Pulling onto her street, the reality that I'll have to say good night in just a few seconds sets in. I don't want to go back to my lonely, empty apartment. I don't want to roll over in my big bed, wishing she was curled up next to me. Since we'd started seeing each other, I found myself doing just that night after night, wondering if she felt the same.

We pull into her driveway, the ornate porch light over her front door lighting up the walkway. Without words, I help her out of the car and take her hand, then her elbow, walking her to her door.

"I had a great time tonight," I tell her, leaning in to kiss her.

She stops me, a small, soft hand on my tux jacket. "I ... I was thinking maybe you could come in. If you want to."

I know how big of a step this is for her, so I don't answer with sarcasm or banter like I normally would. "Yes. Yes, I would like that very much."

Demi smiles, fiddling with her keys as she tries to unlock the door. Nerves are fresh and pungent in the air, both from her and I. With that one question came so much weight. I was coming in, but it was much more than that. Complicity. She was saying it would be okay if we went further.

She was giving herself to me, and I was prepared to treat her with the utmost respect and care.

"Do you want a ... drink? A snack, maybe?" Demi fiddles with her keys, she still hasn't set them down.

The small sweater wrap she had on over the dress, that had me trying to hide my erection all night, still hung over her shoulders. Slowly, I walked to her, unbuttoning my tuxedo jacket and then raising my hands. Just before I touch her, I speak.

"Can I touch you?"

"Yes," she breathes, her eyes never leaving mine.

I lay my hands on her shoulders, pushing the fabric of her wrap off so that I can feel the bare skin underneath. Goose bumps zip down her flesh as my fingers lightly graze her collarbone, her neck, her cheek.

"Can I kiss you?" I gulp, because restraint is so hard in this moment but I know I must use it.

"Yes." The answer is a moan.

Her foyer is dim, nothing but the one light she left on in the living room showing us the way up the stairs. I dip my head, taking her lips slowly and methodically. I want to emblazon my mark on her, so gently and so calculating that years from now she'll touch her lips in a meeting at work and think of this very moment.

After what seems like an eternity of exploring her mouth, I pull back, my vision hazy and my cock as hard as a steel pipe.

"Can I take you to bed?" I wanted to make love with her between the sheets, properly.

"Yes." It seems to be the only logical thought Demi can make right now.

I lace my fingers through her hand, climbing the stairs slowly, not knowing where I'm going but leading anyway. She's relying on me to do this right, and do it right I will.

Before we enter her bedroom, a cream and white paradise that screams of her and smells like almond and vanilla, I wrap her in a hug. My eyes peer down at her, trying to look into her soul.

"I'm going to ask you before I make any move. I want your permission, I want you to be right there with me, knowing full well what you want and what you want to give to me."

She nods, and I can see her pupils dilate and go cloudy. Lust has already stolen over her like fog does to the forest on a dark morning.

Backing into Demi's room, I sit down on the bed facing her. I take off my shoes, unbutton my shirt, unbuckle my belt, all while she watches. She stands there, in that green dress that feels like heaven and looks like hell, her breasts rising and falling with each shallow breath. When I'm naked down to my boxers, I descend on her again, things getting a bit faster.

I nip at her neck, finding the zipper on the dress and pulling it down all the way to the beginning of her pert ass. I push it aside, letting it fall and pool around her feet.

My breath is stolen when I stumble backward, taking in the sight before me. Black lace over creamy skin, begging to be touched.

I lead Demi by the hand, falling backward on the bed. "Straddle me."

She does as I say, her warm, perfect body rubbing up against mine. And then it's on.

My hands are in her hair, her mouth is claiming mine. She's grinding on me like a wanton, needy thing and I can't get enough friction to satisfy my aching cock.

Her tongue runs over the small diamond stud in my ear, sending a jolt to my balls that has me flipping her onto her back.

I run my hands down her sides, and she arches her back. I smell the sex on her, and I need to taste it. Moving down the bed as she wriggles beneath my hands that mold to her, I find her center and pull off her thong, sending it flying across the room.

"Can I taste you?" It's a groan.

"Paxton ..." It's as much of a yes as she can give, and I take the opening.

Feast. Devour. Claim. That is all that registers as I taste her, memories assaulting me. I forgot how sweet she was. Is. I forgot all of her quirks, the things that used to drive me wild and coming back for more.

"I need to be inside of you. Tell me I can be inside of you." It's a question, but my voice is so pained with need that it almost sounds like a command.

"Yes. Yes."

I don't reach for a condom, something I would usually do. We'd moved past those in college, and damn me, I wanted to be inside of her bare. It was a pig move, but she had to be on the pill.

And if she wasn't ... who cared. The thought registered before my brain had time to catch up to it ... but it was the right thought. I was serious about Demi, so serious that nothing was a consequence. Everything was only a step in the eventual steps we would take together.

Driving into her, we both sucked in a lungful of air, every synapse registering pleasure.

"Oh my God ..." Demi moaned quietly, while I tried to get a grip on my spinning vision.

So good. So good. It's the only thing I can think as I stare down at her, my body worshipping hers and vice versa.

Each moan. Each breath. It takes me back to a time so long ago, when I barely knew what I was doing. Memories flood me, the feeling of familiarity gripping my balls tight.

But there is also a newness there, excitement tingling in each bone, muscle and tendon.

Demi unravels just seconds before me, gripping onto me and latching her lips around my neck, almost trying to claw her way through her orgasm. I remember this, her need to get as close to me as possible when she imploded.

And then I see stars, dancing brilliantly before my eyes, encasing Demi in a sea of fireworks as my body empties into hers.

DEMI

Eight Years Ago

Football season was over.

I knew it because I'd heard the kids shouting through campus, drunk students cheering about winning the championship and bowing down to the players as if they were Gods.

And Pax was coming around more, texting me almost every other night, winding up in my bed more often than usual.

"I'm going to New York in two weeks." His fingers danced through my hair, his chest sweaty as I laid on it post-coitally.

The combine. He'd talked about it numerous times, not really to me in a discussion, but more bragging about himself.

That's typically how he spoke to me ... as if I wasn't even really needed in the conversation. I was becoming jaded, after two years of this back and forth, I was just tired. I felt well beyond my meager twenty-somethings. I felt used. I felt exhausted.

I nodded, hating myself for laying here with him again.

"They think I'm going to run the fastest forty yard dash in the last fifteen years." Pax is bragging, puffing out his chest.

"Uh huh." All I was thinking about was what would happen if he left our college.

And me.

"Do you think we'll keep in touch?" I dared to ask the question, because at this point, I seriously had nothing to lose.

He wasn't mine, so in essence, I couldn't lose him. He'd never been mine ... I was realizing that now.

"Of course, babe." Those baby blues looked so deeply into mine.

I could never tell if Pax was lying, or if he really just believed his own bullshit.

A month and a half later, I watch him on my television. ESPN has his face plastered all over their promos ... the anchors on the draft show are discussing how high he'll get picked and gushing over his stellar combine performance.

I didn't see him before he left, his trip to New York coming quickly. He'd come over to fuck me four days before that, and I hadn't heard a peep since. Pax hadn't been back to campus, and the two text messages I'd sent wishing him luck and then to see how he was doing had gone unanswered.

I watch as the team in Boston picks him first, in the first round. The crowd roars, and they show Pax and his parents and his brother all hugging on camera. His petite, sweet looking mother is jumping up and down, crying with joy.

And I'm so happy for him, despite my better judgement not to be. I cry, because I know this is his dream.

But I also want to sob, because I'm not there to share it. Over the course of two years, I'd turned myself inside out for Paxton Shaw. I'd learned about him, worshipped his body, exposed every emotional, raw nerve to him. And he could barely even remember my last name.

I broke, anguished tears leaking onto my cheeks for all of the time I'd lost. For everything we would never be.

I would never sit in front of those TV cameras with him, jumping for joy with his family at his accomplishments. I would never chew on my fingernails in the wives and girlfriends section at his first professional game. I would never hold his hand after a loss.

I would never wear his ring, dress our children up in his jersey number.

Those things were a stretch ... but I had been invested. In love. It was something I couldn't help, once you met Paxton Shaw and were intimate with him, it had to be inevitable. He had that kind of persona ... the one where the moon and the stars would fall in love with him even if they could only see him in the dark of night.

He'd left, and he wasn't coming back.

And so in that moment, I vowed to never speak his name again.

I vowed to forget about him, and harden my heart so that this would never happen again.

The sun set over my backyard, the glass of wine I'd poured collecting condensation on the muggy, oddly humid autumn night. I traced it with my finger, ruminating in my thoughts as I picked it up and sipped.

Maya stirred at the sound of an errant goose in the sky, but immediately lay back down, too lazy and tired to inquire more into the matter.

I might be relaxing, a thick hardcover mystery novel resting on the patio table in front of me, but my head and heart were far from it. I had read the same line over and over, almost fifteen times, before putting it down with a sigh.

Things were getting serious with Paxton, and I was dead scared.

The way he'd introduced himself as my boyfriend. Met my parents. Stayed the night. Worked his way inside me, both mentally and physically. It was all too much.

I was spiraling, didn't know which way to turn or think. So, I'd resorted to self-preservation, dodging his calls and avoiding seeing him for a week.

Paxton was getting too close, and I could feel my hackles

going up. I could feel every instinct inside of me springing into action, mounting an army of anxiety and self-destruction against him, and myself. I couldn't explain it to him, didn't want to ruffle feathers or stop what we had going on. Last time, he'd left me without so much as a "see ya later," and I'd been devastated for longer than I cared to admit.

And just like that, I was the same basket case who had been jerked around by him for two years during college. I wanted him, but I didn't want him. I was in love with him, madly and blindly, but I also knew just how irrevocably I could be hurt if I admitted that to him. I wanted us to be together, but years of systematic rejection had wounded me so deeply that I still hadn't dug myself out of the hole.

Pax had done damage to me all those years ago, and I still wasn't sure he quite saw that. And until I addressed it, I wasn't sure that I could move past it with him.

But for now, instead of acting like a big girl and confronting it, I was hiding in my backyard, or at my office. I'd made excuses to get out of dates, faked headaches and late nights at work to avoid seeing him. My body craved him, but my brain was shouting alarm bells. So I stayed away.

Taking another drink of my Riesling, I picked up my phone and called the one person who I knew would give me a straight answer.

"Hey, sweet cheeks." Chels picked up on the second ring.

"What're you up to?" I kicked my feet up onto the empty chair next to me.

"Watching *Dexter* reruns in my apartment with a sleeve of Oreos." She was nothing if not brutally honest at all times.

"So, we're really working on that date-ability rating." I smiled, wishing I lived closer to my best friend.

"You know it. What's up with you?" I hear her munch an Oreo.

Sighing, I want her to guess. To pull it out of me. So I give the famous, one-word answer that every girl does to let someone know that something is wrong.

"Nothing."

Immediately, I can feel Chels sit up straighter on the other end. "Demi, what's wrong?"

I sigh again, feeling better that she brought it up. "I have to tell you something."

"You're dating Paxton Shaw." Her tone isn't mad, but it isn't happy.

Meanwhile, I'm about to go into cardiac arrest from the shock of her sentence. "Wha ... how did you know?"

"There is a picture circulating on some gossip sites online of the two of you at your annual gala. It labels him as your boyfriend, and you as his girlfriend."

I practically choke. I couldn't handle just myself knowing that I was dating and sleeping with Paxton Shaw. I needed some download time, and now the whole world knew? My level of anxiety went through the roof.

"Why didn't you say anything the minute you found the picture?" I don't want her to be upset with me.

"Because you're a grown-ass woman and I figured you'd fess up sooner or later. I'm not going to say I'm happy, Dem, but I know you need to make your own choices."

I knew that she was the right person to call, for that specific reason. Chelsea was going to be honest, not friend honest. Not that white lie bullshit that sort-of friends did, but the deep, brutal kind of evaluation that left you with the only answer or solution that made sense.

"It's ... different this time, Chels. He's pursuing me. Making promises. Sending flowers and chocolates every week. Wooing me. He met my parents."

"Paxton Shaw meeting the parents, that's something I never thought I'd see. And how did they seem?"

"Well, you know I never told them about him, Chels. That was back in the days when I wasn't a dried up old shrew, and they would have beat me with the Torah for going out with a gentile." And my mother would have killed me for being so weak.

I hear her cackle. "You're not a dried up old shrew. But I appreciate the theatrics."

I smile. "Thank you. But, of course, they loved him. Everyone loves him. He's Mr. Mayor, man about town, the charming gentleman. Even my dad was joking with him by the time Shabbat was over."

I could practically hear Chelsea's eye roll through the phone. "Of course. You know I could still skin that guy alive for what he did to you back then?"

"I could too." I sighed. "But ... I don't know. He's so different, he's been through ... hell, I don't know how he survived what he's been through."

"His parents, right?"

Again, shocked. "How did you know about that?"

"Demi, everyone in the United States knows about that. It's just your fault you aren't like the rest of us rowdy Americans and sit glued to your TV every Sunday from September to February."

"Fine. But yeah, his parents. And I'm not the same." At least I didn't think I was.

"Have you slept with him?" There was the question I'd been waiting for.

"Yes ... and I haven't called him for a week since." I bite at my lip, nervous to hear what she's going to say.

For a few moments, she is dead silent. And then she speaks.

"I think that shows how much you have matured. You know

to preserve yourself, to be weary of him and everything he did. But ... I also think he has changed. At least I'll trust you as a grown-ass woman to know when a person has really changed their stripes. And you've obviously pursued this, you need to see where it leads. Let's face it, you haven't been happy in years. Possibly since the last time you saw him. Every guy you date, you compare to him, am I right? I'm not saying I like it, but I think you know that this might be the big one. And if it works out, I'll be rooting for you both. But ... if he fucks up again, I'll chop his dick off."

I can't help but laugh, the sound freeing. And with it, goes all the nerves that were rumbling around in my stomach.

"Deal. But if things do work out, can you just leave his genitalia where it is? I kind of like it."

Chels makes a vomiting noise. "Gross."

25

PAXTON

I know that Demi is avoiding me.

From the moment I was inside of her again, she's backed away. We woke up the next morning, with her enveloped by my arms and legs, our limbs molded together, and I could feel the distance she was building between us.

All week, my calls had gone unanswered. My flowers met with not even a thank you text. Demi was retreating, and I had to get her back, take her by the hands and lead her through her fear.

It was a miracle she'd agreed to swing by my place tonight. I'd kept it casual, saying that I was having a beer and watching the game, and would she want to swing by. It was something I would have said all those years ago back in college, to get her to come over and hook up. Was that why she went for it? I hated myself for putting things so nonchalantly, because that was absolutely not the case of how I felt about Demi.

I setup on my rooftop, letting the night sky calm my nerves. I could feel a storm brewing between us. Old Paxton would have left it alone, choosing to ignore and avoid it. But present day me knew I had to confront it head on.

"Hey, stranger." I crossed the rooftop patio when I heard the door swing open.

I'd texted Demi instructions on how to get up here, because I wanted to show her this. Maybe it would relax her, maybe I could have this one thing to my advantage.

"Hi. It's beautiful up here." She let me kiss her cheek, but her eyes remained focused on the sky.

"I know, it's half the reason I rented this place. Look, you can see the little dipper right there." I wrapped an arm around her shoulder, gently nudging her chin to look to the right area of the sky.

"Oh, how nice." She went stiff in my arms.

"Demi ..." I tried not to say it sternly, but I couldn't help it. I was annoyed that she was boxing me out.

She moved out of my embrace, and I huffed, annoyed.

"I know you're avoiding me. Are we going to talk about it, or are you going to act like a child?" My temper got the best of me.

"Ha! Me? Act like a child? That's rich, Paxton." She scoffs.

"Yes, you're throwing my past in my face. Again. Can we talk about it like adults? Or are you going to dodge my phone calls?" I should put a lid on it, but I can't.

"Then let's talk about it." She stomps her foot, and I have to bite back a smile.

Even in an angry, exasperated state, she's drop dead gorgeous.

"You still aren't open to me. No matter how hard I try, I see it. All of your walls are still up, you're not giving this a real chance." I point at her, accusing her.

Demi makes an anguished noise and throws her hands up. "And why do you supposed that is, Paxton? Come on, it's not rocket science! What you did to me was psychological warfare. You warped my mind, tortured my heart. For two years you strung me along, like a mouse chasing a piece of cheese she was never going to get. You knew it too, summoning me night after night. You knew you were never going to commit, and yet I'd come running when your crooked your finger. That is cruel and unusual punishment. So excuse me if I'm not over it, if I'm never able to forget it. A person doesn't just forget the dismantling of their heart, ventricle by ventricle."

I ache, because there is nothing I can do to go back and undo all of the hurt that I caused her. But apparently, nothing I've done in the past few months has helped at all. I want to go to her, touch her, but I hang back.

"I've admitted that I was a horrible person to you back then. I was a cocky, selfish, abusive asshole who knew the power he had over you and chose to use it anyway. But Demi, you know what I've been through. How losing my parents changed me. How it made me see that life isn't just all fun and games, that to make it mean something, you need to surround yourself with people that matter."

She walks across the roof, unable to look at me. Her brown hair glistens in the setting sun, and her slim shoulders shiver in the chill that dusk brings.

"I understand that, Paxton. But you also have to understand that a person doesn't just easily forget that. That just because you had a life-altering event rock your world and change who you are as a person, doesn't mean I experienced that with you. I was still here, sitting with my hurt, nursing it like a wound. You have to allow me to have that, to heal in my own time. And I'm trying, but you have to bare with me if I can't automatically and openly give my all to you."

Demi turns around, her eyes guarded. "Do you know that I was engaged? About four years ago, my boyfriend asked me to marry him and I said yes. Only ... I couldn't even book a venue. I had a ring on my finger less than a month before I took it off. I knew he wasn't the one, yet I was trying to force happiness because I thought if I talked myself into it, it would actually become real."

Anger, at myself, ricochets through my bones. Jealousy, that she wore another man's ring, is like an arrow through my heart. "Because deep down, you know you have feelings for me still. And it might suck that you do, but it's true. And I've been going insane trying to prove that I am worthy of you now. I might not have said it back then, but I'm crazy about you, Demi. I was a fucking moron, a clueless college jock with an ego the size of Texas. It took me a long time to set my priorities straight. And they're set straight on you. I didn't realize you were the one who got away until it was too damn late."

A sob bursts from her lips, but she holds a hand up when I try to comfort her. Here we are, two broken people standing under the most beautiful of night skies. How disappointed are my parents of me if they're up there listening?

"I think I should go home." Demi moves towards the entrance to the stairs.

I walk to her, putting a hand to her elbow. "I think you should stay. Even if you don't want to talk, its late. Stay. I'll sleep on the couch, in the guest room ... wherever you want me to. Just stay."

We're at a standoff, when all I want to do is kiss her. "I promise, Demi, I won't try a thing. I just ... I want to be in the same place as you."

"I'm going to regret this, aren't I? Damnit, fine ... but I'm locking the door." She moved to the stairs that led back down to my apartment.

26

The smell of freshly brewed coffee permeates the air when I step out of Paxton's guest room.

My mouth waters, and I realize I'm like one of those Pavlovian dogs. If Paxton is my weakness, then coffee is my drug. I'm one of those people who could drink a whole pot and still go to sleep. My tolerance has become so high that I now drink it black, the bitter grounds fueling my veins when I get to the bottom of the cup.

In the two months since we'd begun seeing each other ... again, I had refused to come here. Call it post-traumatic stress disorder from all the late-night booty calls in college, in which I'd walk by myself through the dark campus over to his dirty, groupie-filled house.

I didn't want to seem like the one who needed him this time around, so I'd always have him pick me up from my place, or meet on neutral ground. The night of the gala was the first and only time I'd allowed him to stay over. And now I was here, in the one place I'd feared going. Even though Paxton's house was now a beautiful, industrial-but-cozy three-bedroom sprawling apartment overlooking downtown Charlotte.

He's standing at the stove in gray sweatpants that show the grooves of his muscled ass underneath, and a plain navy blue T-shirt. His blond hair is tousled and sleep worn, the longest pieces tucked behind his ears. The small stud in his left ear is a black stone today, and it flashes me back to when I suckled on the lobe just a week and a half ago.

Internally, I shush my lady parts, which were all too aware last night that this sexy piece of man meat was asleep just feet down the hall. I had taken the guest room, while Pax had closed the door to his room with a disappointed sigh. I'd left the door unlocked, half-hoping that he'd come in in the middle of the night, and half-hoping he wouldn't.

It turns out, both of my wants were met. Not intending to sleep over, I had nothing but the casual jeans and blouse I'd worn over here the night before. When I'd awoken, in my underwear, there was a T-shirt and shorts laying on the chair in the corner of the guest room. Which meant Pax had come in, but he had honored his promise not to touch me.

The clothes were swimming on me, but it was more comfortable than eating breakfast in jeans, and I loved the smell of him.

"Good morning," I said shyly, feeling out of place in his kitchen.

Pax turns, and a bright smile paints his face. "Good morning. I like you in my clothes."

His eyes roam my body, and I feel like he just lit me like a match. I shuffle my feet. "Thanks ... what're you making?"

Pax moves to the coffee pot, pouring me a mug, and walks it over to me. "Sit, I'm serving you this morning. Eggs and bacon ... I'm not a fancy cook but I think they're pretty good."

"Smells great." I'm not really functioning until I gulp down my first cup, so I start drinking coffee.

"How did you sleep?" He peers over his shoulder at me, scrambling the eggs.

"Well ... thanks for convincing me to stay over. It's nice to wake up and see you." I need to make an effort, to open myself to him.

Our fight on the roof played over and over in my head as I watched the ceiling in the dark last night.

Pax walks over, on a mission, and bends down to kiss me. We've both been yearning for it, I can feel it in the urgency of the kiss. He cups my face and I tug on the strands of his hair. I needed this, an affirmation that things were going to be okay between us.

He was right, I had to let this go. I had to give us a fresh start ... and even Chelsea agreed that if I wanted to take a stab at it, like she wanted to at Paxton, that I should take the leap.

I pull back, taking a minute to smile at Pax.

"You wanted me to try to be more open with you, and ... I'm going to try. Starting now." I take a sip of coffee before I begin. "I believe that all dogs go to heaven. I believe that chocolate is just as good of a medicine as any drug. I believe that Sundays should be spent in bed, and that the calmest place on earth is sitting in a rocking chair, listening to the ocean after dark. I believe that the book is always better than the movie, that you should open only one gift on each night of Hanukkah, none of this massive one-night present bonanza. And I believe that everyone is entitled to one big mistake in their life. And you ... you used yours already. So please don't hurt me again."

He nods. "I won't. I promise. Now, I want to hear more, but I think I'm burning our eggs so I'm gonna pause you for just a minute."

Racing back over to the stove, he finishes up cooking our breakfast before bringing over two heaping plates.

"This is enough food to feed about six people ..." I stare down at my plate.

"We're learning about each other, so learn about me. I eat

roughly four thousand calories a day, and I am a man who loves breakfast food. Therefore, I will always give you way more than you can eat, and I'll probably end up eating off your plate."

Giggling, I dig in, because apparently fighting and then making up leaves me with a huge appetite. We banter over the breakfast table, and I can't help but feel like I'm in the first good place I've been in in many years. I'm happy, but more than that ... I'm content. Wholly comfortable and satisfied just sitting here in Paxton's clothes, with him, chatting and munching on bacon.

When we're finished, and I'm sipping my fourth cup of Joe, I bring up the one subject I've never really spoken to anyone, besides my parents, about.

"I know I mentioned that I love my job, and love helping families and kids in need. But ... I don't think I ever mentioned why it is I started Wish Upon a Star." I collect myself, taking a deep breath.

As if he knows this is serious, Paxton doesn't say anything. Just holds my hands and focuses on me, allowing me to talk.

"I had a little brother, Ezra. He was four years younger than me, with the curliest, darkest hair you've ever seen. He loved toy trucks and was obsessed with trains ... we used to joke that he would be the world's youngest conductor or engineer. When he was seven, he passed away from the same kind of cancer that Ryan has. It took his smile, his energy, his love of all of the things he used to do with it. I was only eleven, and I had no idea how to deal with that kind of loss. For a long time, I couldn't see other children without getting emotional ... my parents had us in family therapy up until I was in high school."

Pax moves his chair closer to me, both of his hands gripping mine now. "Demi, I'm so sorry. I had no idea ..."

I smile, tears in my eyes. "It's okay, and thank you. It still hurts, to this day. But I try ... I try to remember the good times. I keep his picture on my nightstand and his face in my memory.

And that's why I started my company, to give good times back to families like mine. Families who are suffering, who can't remember the fun they used to have. For children who are in pain, who might not have the time or energy that we do. I want to help them, and to honor Ezra. That's a big part of me, and I want you to know it. So ... there it is."

I'd never really talked about Ezra, except to my mother. And talking to someone who lived through his death ... it was different. More emotional. Often, I was a crutch for her, holding her up while she vented her emotions and anguish.

Talking about the good times in his life, about his happy moments ... it felt cathartic. The smile that stretched my mouth was genuine and giddy. I missed him terribly, but I was also so thankful to have had him as a brother.

"Thank you. Thank you for telling me, for letting me know you in this way. I think you're so brave, and incredible to give these families just a little bit of hope back. The fact that you can watch these children go through what your brother did ... I don't know if I could be so strong."

Pax pulls me into his lap, and I curl into him, basking in the warmth of his hug. He rests his chin on top of my head, and we listen to the sounds of the city outside the window.

I don't think I've ever been in a more perfect moment.

"So I said to the girl doing my manicure, I like them rounded, not square!"

A bunch of the girls surrounding the woman telling her story cackle, as if it's the most absurd thing they've ever heard.

I roll my eyes, realizing that maybe this section isn't all it's cracked up to be.

For the first time in my life, and in my knowing Paxton Shaw, I am officially sitting in the wives and girlfriends section. An exclusive club, the manicured, dyed, waxed women around me have baited and hooked professional athletes, and their diamonds and designer sunglasses are a testament to that.

I wasn't aware that it was "uncool" to wear your player's number or any kind of gear for that matter, and so here I sit. In a Cheetahs T-shirt and jeans, with my favorite white canvas sneakers. Most of these women are in leather pants, heels, or some kind of revealing blouse. I feel like such an outsider, but am so happy just to have had Pax ask me to sit here for him today that I'm grinning and bearing it.

"Don't listen to those hags. We call them the WAGS." A

pretty redhead sits down next to me, her attire more casual than the group in front of me.

"Oh, you're not a player's wife?" I thought this section was only for family.

"No, I am. Number eighty-seven, Charles West, that's my man!" She whoops her fist and whistles. Some of the other girls turn around to look at her, disdain in their eyes. "But I'm a wife. Dedicated to my husband's career and helping him grow, while also raising our family and being an independent woman. Those ... those are WAGS. Girls who just want the title and money of dating a professional athlete."

"Ah, gotcha." I breathed a sigh of relief that perhaps there were some normal women if I was going to be sitting here. "I'm Demi ... I'm here for, or I guess with, I don't know. But um ... Paxton Shaw. That's who I'm here to see."

She holds out a hand for me to shake. "Hillary, nice to meet you. I can tell you're definitely not a WAG. Stick with us, you'll be fine."

Hillary points to two girls sitting next to her, and they introduce themselves as Willow and Nicole. I wave, feeling a bit more comfortable than I previously had.

"So, you're all married to players?" I ask, trying to find out a little more about the women I'll probably be spending some time with over the next year.

"Yep. Willow married Bradley, he's on the defensive line, a year ago. And Nicole has been with Jacob, the backup quarterback, for about seven years. And me ... Charles and I are high school sweethearts. Almost thirteen years together, but only eight married."

"Wow." I couldn't imagine being with someone that long, but it sounded nice.

"How about you? Pax was just signed here; did you move with him?" There is no judgment in Hillary's kind brown eyes, just curiosity.

I scratch my head. "Um, no ... we actually kind of used to know each other in college, I've been in Charlotte ever since. When he moved back, we started seeing each other. We've been dating about two months."

Willow leans over. "Wait a minute, you're Demi Rosen ... you organized that wish day for the little boy with cancer a few months back. I know you! You're the CEO of Wish Upon a Star!"

Her voice carries, and the pack of WAGS looks back, studying me for the first time.

I blush, because I don't like to be the center of attention. "Um, yeah ..."

"Oh, girl, you do the work of God. Seriously, I bow down to you. What you do for those families is so amazing." Hillary touches my arm, and I can't stop blushing.

I don't do what I do for the recognition, and it's awkward for me when I'm praised for it. "Well, we just do it for the children, that's all."

Nicole and Willow smile at me, and Hillary keeps chattering away, moving onto the next subject.

The game is intense, especially from the great seats that are designated as the family section. Pax scores two touchdowns, pointing up at me both times he makes it into the end zone. I can't help but blush as Hillary jabs me with her elbow, pointing me out as his "boo." In the end, they win, bringing their record to nine and one.

After the game, the girls bring me to wait with them in a room that has a full spread of food, a fully stocked bar, and dozens of people waiting for the players to come up out of the locker room. Kids run around, playing tag while their mothers sipped wine or spoke to staff from the stadium or front office.

And then finally, big burly men in impeccable suits start to emerge. One after another, greeted by squealing kids or happy wives, kissing and hugging.

Paxton walks in toward the middle of the pack, his hair still damp and curling up past his neck. The dark blond stubble on his chin has a few errant water droplets, and his gray suit brings out the blue in his eyes. I want to drool, or straddle him, but I refrain from both. Instead, I give him a shy wave and wait for him to walk to me.

But he doesn't walk, he runs. Straight at me, until he's in front of me, picking me up around the waist and gripping the back of my neck so that I'm forced to kiss him. The meeting of our mouths sends shockwaves straight to my core, and if we weren't in a room full of people, and children, I would start undressing him right here.

A couple of wolf whistles break me out of my Paxton lust-haze, and I hit his shoulder, signaling for him to put me down.

People are still clapping and staring, and I bury my head in his chest. "You are too much."

"Sorry, I've just never had a woman waiting in the family room for me. Feels pretty damn good ... especially since it's you that is waiting for me."

"So, you can finally call me your girlfriend, huh?"

I think back to the time of a bet, one that hurt me so bad when I found out about it. He wouldn't say it back then ... but he was saying it now. I had to focus on that.

"You know it, baby. And I'm your boyfriend. Hey, I like how that sounds." Pax kisses me again. "Did you have a good time?"

I nod as Paxton laces his fingers through the ones on my left hand and pulls me over to the food line. If breakfast last week was any indication, he had to be absolutely famished after expending that much energy during the game.

"I did. Met some very nice ladies. Hillary West. She's very

down to earth; kind." I look around the room, spotting Hillary as she smacks a kiss on the man who must be Charles.

"That's what I've heard ... good, I'm glad you met someone you can talk to since I want you at every single game from now on. You're my lucky charm." Pax piles chicken, mashed potatoes, salad, and more onto a plate.

"Paxton, you've played in the league for eight years, and I don't know much, but I know that you have a ring, or maybe more. I am not your lucky charm." I put my hands on my hips.

He walks us to a table, setting down his plate and kissing me on the nose. "Yes, you are. No more arguing. I'm so hungry that I could pass out."

"You're nuts ... this is enough food to feed the entire team." I roll my eyes, taking a french fry off of his plate and popping it in my mouth.

Pax smiles. "That's why there is a whole other dining room. What, you didn't think this was the only food, right? We'd all starve!"

G rowing up, I had celebrated Christmas. My parents were never devoutly religious, hell, we never even really went to church. But, every December twenty-fifth, we had a tree up in our living room and left cookies out for Santa.

I'd never been part of a family who believed in something holy, just the trademark Toys "R" Us traditional family that bought into the marketing ploy of the holiday and not the actual meaning. Not to say that our traditions were bad or that I lacked for anything, but being around Demi's family during Hanukkah was a whole different experience.

Aaron put on his yarmulke, placing the traditional cap on his head and opening his prayer book. Sarah carries loads of food on China platters into the dining room of their home, even though it is only the four of us. Matzo ball soup, brisket, gefilte fish, kugel, latkes, and so much more. Demi sets the special Hanukkah chalices on the table for us to drink out of, candles lit everywhere with the beautiful gold menorah in the middle of the table.

"Tonight, we gather for this feast to celebrate the first night of Hanukkah. To celebrate the plight of our people, to remember all that it is to be of the Jewish faith," Aaron starts, going through the prayers by memory as he smiles around the table.

I can feel the energy of their belief in the room, and I'm honored that they're letting me take part. There is actually a real difference in having a holiday that is more about the spiritual side of things, and not just a massive unwrapping of presents.

The prayers that they recited, holding hands and singing, were intricate and they had me a little bit mesmerized. I couldn't understand a lick of it, but with the ambiance and the recitation, I could just feel the love and faith circling around the room.

When they were done, and Aaron had blessed the meal to eat and cut the challah bread, Demi turned to me.

"So, what did you think about your first night of Hanukkah?" She looked gorgeous with her hair pulled off her face, her big eyes shining brightly.

"I think it's amazing." I squeezed her hand under the table.

"You don't have to bullshit just to impress my daughter, Paxton." Aaron spoke up from where he sat across from me.

Now I knew why all those teenage boys were scared that their girlfriend's fathers were going to whack them with a shotgun on the front porch. Because I had a feeling, that if Demi turned her back, Aaron would do the same to me.

"No, sir, and I mean it. Also, Sarah, this brisket is delicious." Maybe if I stuffed my face the entire meal, he wouldn't cut my fingers off for touching his daughter.

"Oh, thank you, sweetheart. Eat, eat, everyone," she clucks, and it reminds me of my mother.

It feels nice to have a holiday with a family for the first time in a while. Usually, my brother, Dylan, and I celebrated holidays three days late because of my football schedule. And we had takeout and bottles of beer while giving each other one single gift. It was rather depressing, and we both missed our parents so much that it overshadowed the day.

"Thank you for letting me be here. It's nice to have a family holiday." I squeezed Demi's hand again.

They all looked at me, and Sarah's eyes became misty. "Well, thank you for being here. It's been a long time since we've been a complete family unit, and I'm happy that you make Demi happy."

Aaron didn't have a backhanded comment for that one, and I counted that as a point for me.

"Oh, Mom, I started reading that new Nora Roberts book, it is so good!" Demi sips some of her grape wine and looks across at Sarah.

"I have to buy it on my Kindle, but I was going through some of the reviews on Amazon and they are wonderful. That Nora just knows how to write them." Her mom cut into an asparagus spear.

"Personally, I don't see how you two read that cheesy crap. Dan Brown is the best writer of this generation." Aaron shook his head.

I cut in, not thinking before I opened my mouth. "That's debatable. He's good, but I prefer Douglas E. Richards."

I'm too busy cutting my food to notice the silence, but when I look back up, they're all staring at me.

"You read science fiction?" Aaron is gaping at me.

"I didn't realize you ... liked books." Demi practically jokes.

I smile, goading them. "Oh, so what? The jock can't like to read? That's a bad stereotype, guys."

Sarah cackles. "Oh, sweetheart, you are something else. A pleasant surprise around every corner! Well, good. We can start a book club then."

Aaron butts in. "I love Richards ... he's one of my favorite authors. Which is your favorite novel?"

I mentally high five myself for being a science fiction nerd, because it's totally scoring me points with my future father-in-law. And yeah, I went there. I was cocky enough to believe it would come true.

"*Mind War*, hands down. But they're all good."

Aaron launched into a conversation with me about his novels, and Sarah and Demi began to talk about a show on Netflix that fictionalized the British monarchy.

It was a night of family, of a little too much wine and getting to know each other on a deeper level. Sarah brought out dessert and set gold chocolate coins called gelt down by mine and Demi's plate. Apparently, it was a tradition to give the children to bring them luck and good fortune.

By the time Demi and I said good night, I felt like I was really being accepted into the fold. And as she held my hand on the car ride home, I felt the weight of that chocolate coin in my pocket.

I already had all of the luck and good fortune I needed.

We're lying on the couch, the sun going down outside, with Maya curled beneath our feet.

"Why do you watch this asinine show again?" Pax is snuggled into me, my body being the big spoon.

"Because I love love. And it's mindless drama and sometimes a girl just needs her guilty pleasure. Now shush or you can't stay here and watch." I turn my attention back to the TV, watching as twenty-five women vie for one man's attention.

"But your boobs make nice pillows." The large man eclipsing my couch snuggles even harder, making me giggle.

If someone were watching right now, they'd laugh at how big of a baby this macho football player actually was.

This is how we've spent the last month. Paxton all but moved in with me, taking Maya out on a morning run right after I pull out of the driveway, them trying to race me to the end of the street before my car turns left toward the city. I cook us dinner and sit with the wives at Sunday games. He makes the right side of the bed, at my insistence, and I have learned not to leave the toothpaste on the counter because it drives him nuts.

I'm not sure when we fell into this routine, this suburban

fairy tale ... but I am in heaven. Freaking love it. I haven't told him that; I'm so scared to use the *L* word that I practically jump out of my skin every time I think it.

Over the past month, we've blended our lives ... and somehow made them even better. We've given us the chance to be a team, a real shot at a relationship, and damn, we've all but knocked it out of the park.

The guy on TV asks one of the girls about past relationships and sets off a lightbulb in my brain. They're talking about exes, and you can tell that the guy is doing nothing but checking out her boobs while she prattles on about a five-year relationship she just got out of before coming on the show.

Red alert, buddy.

I turn to Pax, sometimes hating the cheesy drama of this show. "So, you know about my history while we were apart. Broken engagement and all that. How about you? You can't tell me that there weren't any ladies in your life."

When we were ... whatever we were in college, I used to torture myself. Stalk his Facebook page to see who he was hanging out with, and if any girls tagged him in a picture. I can't help but do it now, wondering if he had any serious relationships in the time I didn't know him.

Pax ruffles my hair, snuggling in closer. "Oh no, we're not going there."

"What?" I laugh. "I'm not going to judge you. I don't care."

I so cared.

"Oh, yes, you do care. And it doesn't matter anyway, all of that is in the past. Only forward, remember?"

I rub up against him in a catlike manner, trying to sex information out of him. "Oh, I know. But really, there was no one special?"

Pax sighs, combing his fingers through the ends of my hair. It's distracting and feels good, and he knows what he's doing.

"It doesn't matter if there were a hundred women in my past. I've only ever been in love with one. You. I love you. I'm in love with you." Pax says it so matter of factly, as if we're still talking in jest, bantering back and forth.

I'm stunned, my fingers pausing mid stroke of his arm. "I've waited a long time to hear you say that."

He looks up, his baby blues furthering my paralysis. "And I'm sorry it's taken me so long. I guess you were just lightyears ahead of me in maturity. No, I know you are."

I remove my arms from around him, readjusting so that we can look at each other, face to face. "Yes, I am. Which is why I can admit that I've been in love with you for ten years. Even when you didn't love me back, even when we didn't know each other at all anymore. I can admit that without embarrassment, because they were and are my true feelings. It took a lot to get to this place, but … I'm in love with you, Pax. And I'm not scared of it anymore."

He held my face in the palm of his hands. "You don't have to be scared. I'm not going anywhere. I love you."

One of the women on the show interrupts us, giving a dramatic confessional about how madly in love she is with this guy after only a week of knowing him.

"See, we need to take a page from their book. Stop wasting so much time, just admit to loving each other after a week of dating, and then get married after eight weeks." Pax sticks his tongue out at me, erasing the tension of the moment.

It's out there, we've both admitted it and it's like a weight has been lifted. I know that he returns the feelings that I've had for so long.

My heart spikes, though, when he says the word married. We haven't spoken about the future much, have just been focused on the present. Saying those three big words is the most we've committed to a long-term future, but I can't lie and say I haven't fantasized about walking down the aisle to Pax.

I can't lie and say I haven't dreamed of my wedding day since I was a little girl. What the dress will look like, what song we'll dance to. And for ten years, I've dreamed that it would be Paxton Shaw that would say "I do" standing across from me.

"Well, we are way behind then, you better get on it," I joke, snuggling into him before he can use me as the big spoon again.

"Oh, I plan to." Pax kisses the top of my head.

And my heart flutters.

I t might be a cliché, but there really is no place like home.

After my parents passed, I was already making the big money, a professional football salary as a twenty-two-year-old who had no strings and no responsibilities. I'd had enough sense back then, thank God, to know that my parents would want my brother and I to keep the house we grew up in. So, I continued to pay the mortgage until it was paid off, and we came back to visit as often as we could.

Dylan, my brother, lived at our childhood home in the suburbs of Rhode Island in the summers, his technical engineering job allowing him to work from almost anywhere he pleased.

And since it was a bye week, I'd decided to bring Demi up here, show her what cold weather really looked like.

"Snow!" She said it with childlike wonder, as if she'd never seen it before.

"Yes, that's this wet, white stuff that is making it so hard to drive. It comes from the sky," I joke while trying to steer my truck over the wet highway, my tires skidding with each jerk of the wheel.

Demi scoffs. "I wasn't born yesterday, Pax. We just never get snow in Charlotte, it's been years since I've even had to wear a down coat."

Of course, she'd dragged me to the mall the minute I'd invited her to come up here on my weekend off. One thing I had learned about Demi was that she loved an ensemble, and I can't say it wasn't fun watching her pick one. We'd argued about whether or not she'd need a full parka and ski mask; I told her she was going to the Northeast, not the North Pole. She'd delighted in picking out a new pair of Ugg boots, a North Face jacket, and gloves that allowed her to still use her smartphone. She'd been plugged into it the entire drive, and I realized that for her, work never really stopped.

My gift, one of many that I planned to surprise her with this weekend, had been a cream colored winter hat with a puffy pom-pom on top. Demi had squealed when she opened it, clapping at the cuteness.

"Tell me about the hat again?" she asked now, touching the fuzzy ball at the top.

I glanced at her, admiring her stunning profile and then turning my eyes back to the road. "It's from this brand called Love Your Melon, fifty percent of their hats and apparel bought goes toward fighting pediatric cancer."

Demi sighs. "I love that, thank you for getting it for me. You know how special that fight is to me."

I reach over, squeezing her knee. "I do. Now remind me again why we decided to road trip this?"

"Because road trips are fun, and I planned activities, and now we're almost there. Don't tell me you didn't have fun at the aquarium in Baltimore, or that those sandwiches at Harold's Deli weren't to die for."

Okay, she was right ... those sandwiches were fucking delicious. She'd convinced me, when we had first discussed making the trip to Rhode Island, that we should drive it instead of fly. Apparently, my beautiful CEO was not a fan of airplanes, and I was just big enough of a sap to give into her wishes. Plus, she made it sound like fun. And it had been, but it was a lot of driving and my back was starting to hurt and my ass had fallen asleep forty miles ago.

"But this last leg is sooo long, I need something to occupy me. And if you play one more Dave Matthews song, I'm going to scream." Her love for the chilled-out rocker was a tad annoying.

"Fine, what would you like to listen to?" she huffs, and I smile because we sound like an old married couple.

Which is already what I intend for us to be.

"Read me something. Sports trivia, yeah, that'll keep me awake and aware."

Demi laughs. "You just want to impress me with your vast knowledge of men who play with balls."

"I'll show you how to play with balls." I wink and raise my eyebrows in her direction.

For the next hour and a half, Demi reads me sports trivia, of which I ace every question. But I was right, it keeps me alert, and I pull off the highway and onto the streets of Bedford with a contented sigh.

We wind our way through the town, and I point out some of my favorite landmarks to Demi. The high school field where I first fell in love with football. The library that my mother used to volunteer at. The Applebee's that my friends and I used to loiter around at every Friday night, trying to look cool and get half-price appetizers.

And then we finally pull into the driveway of my childhood home.

"Home sweet home." I unbuckle, leaning over to taste Demi's lips. "I've been waiting to do that this entire car ride."

She smiles, and we begin to unpack, emptying the car of

trash and I grab our bags out of the back. I shuffle through my keys and land on the right one, unlocking the front door and breathing in the smell of my parents. Even five years later, it still lingers in every fiber of the house.

I stop on the front mat, just letting the feeling of home sink into my bones. It's bittersweet, being here. Without them, but also remembering every good memory we had here.

Demi walks in and stands beside me, and then notices the gift sitting directly in front of us.

"What is this?" Demi points to the picture in its frame, a bow on the corner.

I set our bags down and send a silent thanks to Dylan for delivering this here so she could see it right when we walked in.

"Take a look." I start to unzip my jacket and shrug out of it, moving to the hall closet. My mom would have yelled if I didn't hang up my coat right away.

Demi walks to the bench in the hall, the same one that has been there since I was a little boy. She bends down, reading the words on the piece of art. It is a midnight blue background in a whitewashed frame, with a large circle in the middle made up of a formation of stars.

"Oh my God ... Pax ..." Her hand moves to her mouth when she realizes what it is.

"It is the exact formation of stars in the night sky on the day that I walked into your office a few months ago. I found it through a company who makes these for any date you have in mind. I wanted to commemorate it, the first time I saw you again and knew what I'd been struggling through all those years for. And you said to me that first week, that all of the children you worked with reminded you of stars who might lose their shine here on earth, but they were watching us from above. I like to think that all those burnt out stars in the sky that day led me straight to you."

She turns to me, tears falling down her cheeks. "This is the most amazing thing anyone has ever given me. Pax ..."

Demi moves swiftly toward me, and I catch her, molding our bodies together. "I love you. I mean it."

"I love you, too," she mumbles into my sweater. Pulling back, she laughs. "You've made me a mess. I'm all emotional now."

"Would you believe that I was half-hoping I could get you to cry? But only good tears?" I kissed her wet cheeks.

"Yes, I would believe that. Your charm outdoes itself again." She rolls her eyes.

"Come on, let's get you out of that jacket. And maybe those clothes." My blood heats, because I've been cooped up in a car for too long and need to stretch my legs. Or my body. Preferably on hers.

"Isn't your brother going to be here soon?" She anxiously looks around.

"Probably, but who cares? He should know not to cockblock."

And with that, I pick her up and sling her over my shoulder, heading for the stairs and up to my childhood bedroom.

"Paxton!" She slaps at my butt, but I hear her laugh.

Yeah, she's definitely not going to care if my brother walks in on us mid-horizontal hula.

B eing invited to Paxton's childhood home is like being invited into a part of his life that I've been dying to know about for a long, long time.

This house, a white colonial with big oak trees flanking the front, with a rope swing tied to one of the thick branches, was something out of a movie. It was picturesque, nestled onto a street in the small lake town that Pax and his brother grew up in.

Photos of the family hung on every wall, with old sunken couches that looked loved sitting in front of a cozy fireplace in the living room. For years, when we were hooking up, I'd wanted to know as much as I could about the Shaw family. I wanted to be introduced, to listen to his mom's stories about Pax as a little boy, to drive up here for holidays and become a part of them.

Coming to this house was like a treasure trove of unanswered questions that I'd always had. But it was also bittersweet, because I was here after his parents had passed. Part of me was a little sour that it had taken Pax so long to realize what we could be together, because he'd wasted time and in doing so, I'd never become close to his parents.

At the same time, I knew he was thinking some of those

same thoughts, and I didn't want to burden him with my small amount of anger.

Over the past two days, I'd met and spent time with Dylan, Pax's brother. He was quieter than his brother, but just like Pax, he had a hell of a charming personality too. It was like the more silent he was, the more you wanted to try to get him to smile. And where Pax was blond, Dylan was dark, with almost jet-black hair and dark, stormy eyes.

Today, all three of us had spent the day on the half-frozen lake near their house, and they'd tried to teach me how to fish. After trying for half an hour and getting no bites and not really understanding the point of the whole thing, I picked up my book and read. It was fun, and even though we didn't say much, it was the companionship that equaled bonding.

And now we were inside, the fire roaring in the living room, while Pax and I cleared the dishes from dinner.

"Dylan really didn't have to stay at a hotel." I felt bad that he'd left, giving Pax and I some alone time.

Although, it was kind of nice, imagining what it would be like if we lived in this big house, filled it with kids, grew old together ...

Pax's voice snaps me out of my daydream. "He's happy to do it, babe ... honestly, I think he's hooking up with one of our old high school friends who still lives here, and he wanted some-where private to go."

"Does he date much?" I wondered if Dylan had the same history with women that his brother did.

Pax shrugs. "Honestly, we never talked about girls much, don't know why. Although he did tell me before that he really likes you. And that if I ever mess things up, he'll cut my nuts off himself. So, thanks, I think my brother likes you better than me."

"As he should." I wink, drying a bowl.

Pax wipes his hands off, the suds slipping into the sink as he hands me the last piece of silverware to dry. I'd insisted on cleaning up the old-fashioned way, something about it just seemed right in this snowy, homey environment.

"I think we need to be done with cleaning dishes." He hugs me from behind, his hands snaking around my waist and his fingers pulling at the waistband of my leggings.

"You're incorrigible." I laugh, because all we've done in the past two days, when we weren't with Dylan, is make love.

Not that I'm complaining, being intimate with Pax again is like biting into a chocolate ice cream cone after giving up ice cream for eight years.

"And? What's your point? Take it as a compliment that I can't get enough of you. You drive me fucking insane, Demi." He growls into my neck, his teeth sinking into the soft skin there.

I can't help the moan that escapes my lips, and I set down the last kitchen item before I break something.

"How do you want me?" I want to hear him detail every dirty thing he's going to do. Pax has always been particularly skilled when it comes to dirty talk.

And tonight, I don't want slow and sensual.

"How do *you* want *me*?" He flips the tables.

I pause, wondering if I can reveal the thing I've dreamt about for so long. I've never had the guts to try it with anyone else ... and I'm not sure why. I don't know why I've been so shy about sex, except with Pax. Maybe he just brings out the side of me that feels comfortable expressing what turns me on.

"Well, there is this one fantasy, or actually we've done it already, that I have thought about many times over the years." I sigh as his lips hit my neck, and my legs wrap more tightly around his waist.

The cold edge of the counter seeps through my leggings, and

it's a scintillating contrast to the way my core is absolutely burning.

"And what is that?"

I blush, even if he can't see it, because thinking about our younger years makes me crazy with lust. We were animals, always drawn to each other.

"Remember the night of the Halloween party at the lacrosse house off campus? They had those Jell-O shots made with Everclear and everyone kept trying to jump off the roof into the pool?"

It had been a wild night, and one that had been hazy in my memory. But lord did I remember going back to Pax's bedroom.

"Oh shit, yeah ... my friend Bobby almost broke his neck doing that." He picks his head up and laughs, and I can see he's been transported back to that night.

"Do you remember what we did that night, in your bedroom?" My smile is devilish, and the tight buds of my breasts tingle with the memory.

I can see the gears working in Pax's brain, and then I see it, the instant they all click. "Fuck ... that was hot. Damn, I'd forgotten about that."

I nod, knowing he is thinking what I'm thinking. "What do you say we give it a try, for old time's sake?"

Pax pushes his hands up inside of my long sleeve T-shirt, making me shiver with need. "I'm not the spring chicken I used to be, babe. I'm an old man now, what if I break a hip."

I scoff. "I think we've tested the limits of those hips recently, and I think you'll be just fine."

His hands travel up, finding their way to my bare breasts, and he rolls each nipple in between his fingers. "You're the finest one in the room."

Lips come at me full force, and I guess I've convinced him,

because we're mauling each other in the middle of the kitchen counter before I know it.

Heat licks up my spine, through the flesh of my thighs, burning my cheeks. Suddenly, my clothes feel too constricting, they're scalding me, and I need them off.

I'm not sure who starts the undressing, but in record time, we've shed all clothing, and I think Pax shreds my underwear in the process. Who knows, who cares. My head is spinning, and all I can focus on is the ball of need pooling low in my core. He is everywhere, biting my neck, sucking my tingling nipples, moving down the counter, his knees hitting the hardwood floor as he spreads my thighs around his head.

"Oh fuck!" I buck off the counter, not even embarrassed by the curse that just left my lips.

He's eating me alive, his teeth scraping against my swollen nub and nearly sending me over the edge. I see his right hand disappear, and then his muscles beginning to work. I realize he's jerking himself, as he feasts on my body, and it's so hot that my orgasm steals over me before I can even take a lungful of air in.

I writhe, gripping the edge of the counter to keep upright, or from collapsing and hurting myself. My climax is white hot, making my vision fuzzy as every limb sings with ecstasy.

I'm barely conscious when Pax stands, grabbing me and moving to the wall. Instinctually, my legs come around his waist, and I press my lips into his neck, awaiting the invasion.

It comes with a burn and two groans of pleasure, echoing through the dark, silent house.

Pax isn't gentle. He impales me, up against that wall, the same exquisite feeling that I felt all those years ago coursing through my body. He whispers in my ear as he fucks me, and that's what it is, fucking.

"Your pussy feels like a fucking vise."

"Scream for me, baby."

"Who is the only one who knows how to fuck you?"

And while he talks dirty to me, he grips my neck, looking me straight in the eyes.

It's lust, but it's also love.

And Paxton is the only man I'll ever feel both for.

"Sweetheart, why don't you change the paint color in here? A nice pop of yellow would really brighten the place up."

My mother walks around my office, examining every nook and cranny. And driving me up the wall that she wants to guilt me into painting sunshine yellow.

"I like my whites and beiges, but thanks, Mom." I turn my head back to my computer, furiously checking for any reason to excuse myself and get back to work.

Every other week, she'd bring me lunch from my favorite Jewish deli near their house, and I loved the food and her company.

For about an hour and a half.

Anything after that and I was grasping at straws to get her to leave. Don't get me wrong, I love my mom to death, but her nagging can wear on me.

My staff has no idea what I'm talking about. Whenever she comes in, she has a hug and a piece of candy for each of them. Sometimes she brings the entire office lunch and regales them with stories that they roll on the floor laughing at.

"Paxton says hi, by the way." She slides this into the conversation as if it's as casual as saying that she's taking up yoga.

I nearly spit out the iced tea she brought for me. "What?"

"Oh, yeah, I stopped over at his apartment earlier to bring him some fresh baked bread that I whipped up yesterday."

It's official, my mother is smitten with my gentile boyfriend.

"Mom, you can't just ..." I laid my head in my hands.

I loved her, would do anything for her. But her nagging and meddling was going to give me a migraine. Not that anything was wrong between Pax and I, but ... I'm not sure. Maybe I didn't feel like bringing anyone too close to us yet, because we *were* enjoying each other's company so much. I wanted to stay in this honeymoon phase a little bit longer, before we started coming home and complaining about work, or traffic, or why there were dirty dishes in the sink.

"What? I don't get what the big deal is, Demi! He's part of your life, so I want him to be part of ours. And he doesn't mind, we sat down and chatted for almost two hours. He told me about his parents, and his retirement ... he's a very sweet boy, you know."

I did know, and I had to smile because my mother could get anyone to talk. She could probably get those stoic guards outside of Buckingham Palace to talk, and it was part of their job description not to. But I also didn't want her finding out about our past, in college. Perhaps one day I would tell her, but not now.

"What did he say?" I was actually genuinely curious about what he'd divulged to her.

"We talked about the accident some, but mostly about what his parents instilled in him as a child. And oh, he definitely wants to have children after he hangs up his cleats this year." She winked at me as if I should start tracking my ovulation cycle in anticipation.

"Mom, oh my God ..." I couldn't do anything but laugh.

"I think you should have three, how wonderful would it be to have all those little *bubbalas* running around?!" She claps her hands together as if she can just picture it now.

I have to admit, I can see it too. A future, a family, with Pax. Little blond-haired boys rough housing in the yard, learning how to play football from their father. A girl who looked just like me, lying in my arms as I read her a book. It sounded like exactly what I wanted out of life.

"That would be pretty wonderful," I tell Mom, because it's impossible not to get swept up in her jubilation.

"That's how I know this is the one. That Pax will be the man you marry." She walks over and kisses me on the nose.

"How?"

"Because even when you're annoyed with me, you still had a smile on your face the whole time. You never did that with Zachary. That's how I know."

My heart warmed, because she could see it too. "I told him about Ezra."

Mom stilled, and then patted me on the shoulder. Her eyes looked out the glass walls of my office building, down onto Charlotte, but I knew she was seeing the son she'd lost.

"Good, you should share that with the person you love. He should know about our baby." Her eyes are misty when she looks back at me.

She pretended not to wipe her eye on her sleeve. "Now then, when is the next time I'll see you both? I think I should lay claim to every single night, put it in your wedding vows. You'll spend them with your father and I, because I'm your mother and I say so."

There was that Jewish guilt again, and Mom was the expert at it.

I stood and enveloped her in a hug, because while she could

be a pest, I loved her fiercely. It was the kind of hug you gave your parent when you realized just how much they did for you, and how life would be drastically different if they weren't the one who raised you.

"Whatever you say, Mom. We'll be there."

33

Watching Pax play in a football game from my couch, the announcers singing his praises on TV, brought me back to my college days.

Only this time, when he scored a touchdown, he did the funny dance move he told me he would perform in this game especially for me. It looked like a bad imitation of Michael Jackson, and each time he did it, for the three touchdowns he scored, I giggled.

They were playing away for the championship game that would secure their place in the Super Bowl, and I was upset I couldn't go, but we were fulfilling an extra special wish this weekend that I didn't want to miss.

One of the cases we'd been working on for a while, granting the dream of a teenage girl with Lupus, had finally come to fruition. She wanted to meet one of Hollywood's It Girl actresses, the same one who was the star of those tween movies about vampires that netted millions at the box office.

I had worked tirelessly to not only make the hang out happen, but it just so happened that a part of the next movie was being filmed in a remote location just outside of Charlotte.

I'd scored her an entire day on set, watching and hanging out with the It Girl while she filmed.

And if I was being honest, I loved the movies too and wanted to be there all day to watch her dream come true and get a little inside information on the next installment.

Paxton understood, but he was upset his lucky charm wasn't going to be there. So, he'd taken a pair of my underwear, sprayed in my perfume, for good luck. I had tried to wrestle them away from him, embarrassed that they would be sitting in his suitcase, but he had insisted.

"Our dirty little secret." He'd winked as he said it, and I had flushed but let him keep them.

I patted Maya on the head as she slept in my lap, all seventy pounds of her, and took a sip of chamomile tea. As much as I missed Pax, it was nice to have a single girl's night by myself. I'd been spending so much time with him, since we were practically living together now, that I missed some of my alone time.

Life was immeasurably better now that Pax was back in it, but I missed being able to sit around in my ugliest, but comfiest, sweatpants, eating pickles wrapped in turkey, or a whole plate of Pillsbury cinnamon buns with no one looking. I missed binge watching *Downton Abbey* marathons, or staying up until four in the morning finishing a good book without someone rolling over and telling me it would be a good idea to go to bed.

And this weekend, I had gotten to do all of those things. It filled my weird single person behavior tank for a while so that I could go on being in a committed relationship without feeling like climbing the walls.

The game ended, the sound of the whistle and a bunch of fans cheering coming from the speakers in my TV. I clapped too, so freaking excited that the Cheetahs won and that Pax would be going to the Super Bowl. He deserved this, to go out on the highest note possible.

An hour and a half later, my phone rang, Pax's picture and number flashing on the screen. I'd shamelessly set his photo in my contacts as a shirtless one from a spread in a sports magazine from a couple of years ago. Sure, it might be awkward if it ever rang in a business meeting, but damn did it make me drool while I was in private.

"Are you excited we're going to the Bowl?" Pax sounded so excited.

"Well, I'm more excited that Demi Lovato will be performing the halftime show ..." I teased him.

"Oh, stop! You know you can't wait to wear my jersey and kiss me as I raise that Lombardi trophy." I could hear the wind whip past the speaker of his phone as he walked outside somewhere.

"You played so great, babe. I especially loved the horrible dance moves." I curled my feet under me, getting more comfortable to talk to him for a while.

I missed him.

"You liked that, huh? The press sure did, trying to ask where that little bit of spontaneity came from. I miss you, gorgeous." He spoke my inner thoughts.

"I loved it. I love you. I'm so excited! So is Maya, although she slept through the second half of the game. But she sends her love." I look at the dog snoring on the other end of the couch.

"Kiss her for me. I'm back at the hotel now, how about you just fly out and be on the bed when I open the door?" I hear the ding of an elevator in the background.

As much as I had enjoyed being home alone, I was done now. I wanted to be in bed with him, too. "Oh, how I wish. But we can stay on the phone all night. And you'll be home in the morning."

I hear the automatic lock of a hotel room door, and then the closing of one. "But I'm alone in my hotel room and I'm horny."

My thighs suddenly felt like I needed to rub them together, like tingles were moving through my core that I had to alleviate. "Oh, are you?"

"I am. Getting undressed all alone. In the dark. No one to rub my aching body." I hear Pax unbuckle his belt, the shuffling noise of clothes coming off.

I lean back into the couch, my breasts suddenly aching for his touch. "So, pretend I'm there. Naked, in bed waiting for you."

We've both silently agreed to play this game. It feels a little dirty, a little explicit, and oh so good.

"I'm sliding into bed now, God, Demi, I'm so hard for you."

I'm fully reclined on the couch now, my hand resting on my stomach, quivering there. "Do you want me to touch myself for you?"

"Fuck yes. Put that hand down your pants, baby. Finger yourself and think of me stroking myself here to the sounds of you getting off."

Oh lord, could that man set my skin on fire. I breached the waistband of my pants, gliding my hand down until I felt my slick center.

"Pax," I moan, stroking through my folds the way I know feels good. "Talk to me. What do you want to do to me?"

I hear his sharp intake of breath. "I want to lie you down on the bed, completely naked in the moonlight so that I can see all of that beautiful skin. Your nipples, so hard and ready for me to suck. The scent of your arousal, God, I'd stick my tongue right in there."

My breaths are so shallow, my hand working my swollen nub over and over in a circular motion. "You're making me feel so good, Pax."

"I want you to come for me, baby." His breathing is ragged in my ear. "I'm stroking so hard for you, I'm so close to squirting all of this cum out for you. Just imagine me buried deep inside of you, pounding your pussy—"

His use of that dirty word puts me over the edge, my climax bursting through me like an unfiltered beam of light. Blinding and fast, roaring through my system. The sounds I make are inhuman, not of conscious thought.

As I wind down, I'm acutely aware of Paxton grunting loudly over and over into the phone. After a minute or two of us catching our breath, he speaks first.

"If our phone sex can be that hot, I can't wait to get home to you tomorrow."

I chuckle. "Well, Maya got a hell of a show, that's for sure."

I can hear Pax's smile through the phone. "That's why we always lock her out of our room, can't have the dog cockblocking us."

34

I hit the ground hard, the cold indoor turf hitting my back as I suck in a breath.

"Are you trying to fucking kill us?" Connor dry heaves, collapsing beside me.

"Only trying to get you fucking ready for the Super Bowl. Or do you not want to win a ring?" Anthony cackles, putting his notebook down, and I hope that means we get a bit of a break.

The Cheetahs made the playoffs, and then we made the NFC championship, and then we won. I can't say I'm surprised, our team is really fucking good. But ... there is something in my bones. It feels the same as the three other times I've been in this position, and with the sun setting on my career, some kind of fated feeling is settling over me.

Little does anyone know though, that I'm not coming back next year. Whether we win or lose, I'm hanging up the jersey, I'll have seen my last fifty-yard line.

"Yeah, I want the ring. I also want to be able to walk onto the field in two weeks, too." Connor pouts, gulping down the contents of his water bottle. "Hey, man, congratulations by the way. A little boy, huh?"

Anthony smiles and inclines his head at Connor. "Thanks, bro, we are really excited."

"What's that?" I've been so caught up in Demi that I've missed some of our training sessions, opting to workout on my own to get home to her quicker.

"My wife and I are expecting again, a little boy in June." He beams, and you can feel the pride coming off of him.

"Congratulations, man, that is awesome." I pat him on the shoulder, and inside a pang of jealousy ripples through my stomach.

Not because I want Anthony's life, but because I want to have a child. I shouldn't have wasted so many years, shouldn't have been so selfish. Now I'm retiring, and I feel like I've put my life on hold for this sport with nothing to show for it but some silly rings and bragging rights.

Do I think Demi would go for letting me knock her up tonight?

"Damn, I can't imagine having a kid, though." Connor shakes his head as if I need to explain the birds and the bees to him.

"That's because you are a kid. I can't imagine you having one either." Anthony laughs.

"Like, what do you feed a kid? It's not like a dog, where the food is clearly labeled in the store and you just pour it in a bowl on the floor twice a day. Hell, I can't even do that. It's why I don't have a dog." Connor keeps going.

I have to crack up at that one, because he is so clearly out of his league in this conversation. "Note to self, never ask you to babysit."

"Why, you thinking about getting that fine-ass woman of yours pregnant?" He winks at me.

Actually, it was what I was just thinking about. "Maybe ... in the future."

"Damn, you don't mess around, Shaw." Connor whistles.

Anthony studies me, because he must know the look on my face. "Yeah, he wants to knock her up. Right now, if I'm correct. I'd know that face anywhere; it's certainty. I felt it when I met my wife, and I can damn sure tell that you feel that way about Demi. Just put a ring on it first, I'm a traditional kind of guy."

"Oh, I plan to." I nod, and they both exchange a glance.

What they also don't know, aside from my retirement bombshell, is that I'd spent three hours at the most prominent jewelry store in Charlotte the other day.

Only to leave empty handed because none of the rings had felt right.

I called Dylan and asked him to go into the safe at our parent's home and get Mom's ring. He'd FaceTimed me to show me the ornate, rose gold antique ... a family heirloom passed down through the generations. It had been my mother's engagement ring and had been returned to us when she passed.

I knew right then that it was meant for me to give to Demi. I'd had him send it to me, securely, and the box had arrived just three days ago.

"Well, tell us what the plan is!" Connor semi-shouts, and they must have been staring at me longer than I realized.

"Yeah, give us the romantic details," Anthony chimed in.

"This is what you guys want to talk about in our manly athletic facility, just weeks before the Super Bowl?" I avoided the subject, mostly because I had no idea what I was going to do yet.

They looked at each other, and exclaimed at the same time, "Yes!"

I shifted on the ground, picking a blade of fake grass. "Well, truth be told, I don't know yet."

Looking up, they both had disappointed expressions in their faces.

"Okay, well, what does she like? My wife, for instance, loves ice cream. So, I had a pint made up, planted in the grocery store, and when we went to pick it out one night, I made sure she saw it. Then I got down on one knee right there in the middle of Whole Foods." Anthony smiled.

"Dude, that's actually kind of brilliant. Will they make those for anybody, like even if you're not getting engaged?" Connor looked like he had some sort of idea, and it had nothing to do with marriage.

We ignored him, carrying on our conversation. "I mean, Demi, she's simple. She likes curling up on the couch, reading. I think she'd like for me to do something simple and private, but at the same time, I'd like to announce it to the world. For … past reasons."

No one knew about us hooking up in college. Not that I cared if they did, but it seemed unnecessary to let people all the way into our business like that. However, I still felt guilt about how I treated her back then. And if I could make up for that by announcing to the whole world that I wanted her to be my wife, then I wanted to do it. I wanted to shout from the rooftops that I was in love with Demi Rosen, and that I wanted to spend my entire life with her.

"Sounds shady as fuck, just saying. But, my dude, you have the world on a string this week, you have the perfect stage. Hello, Super Bowl proposal? I'd say you can't go wrong if you whip that diamond out after we win us a ring."

Connor sent me a thumbs-up after speaking his idea, and I had to admit …

It was a damn good idea.

35

I t was surreal, sitting in front of a bunch of reporters for what was going to be one of my last times doing this.

Over the last eight years, I'd been prey for these guys more times than I could count. Trying not to become their next soundbite, trying to liberally dole out my answers in a politically correct way. I'd played the game, and I'd played it well. Both on the field and off. And now it was time to say goodbye.

My knee hadn't been the same, and although I'd played an incredible season, with one more notch to put in my belt before I went, I knew I was done. I could feel it. And while I was sad, I was also looking forward to the next chapter.

I looked to Demi, who was waiting just outside the line of sight of the cameras pointed directly at me, my sole, lonely figure seated at a table in front of the NFL and Cheetah's logos on a blue background. She waved, giving me a thumbs-up and a small smile. My woman, the one person who I'd discussed this with in depth. Yes, my brother knew, but he hadn't been the one staying up with me when I couldn't sleep at two a.m. because I was so confused and anxious about retirement.

It's unprecedented, the fact that the Super Bowl is being held in the same city as one of the team's playing in it. It's only fitting that it will be my last game, with all of the stars aligning.

The team's public relations manager, Angela, walks up behind me and announces that I'll be giving a press conference. Asks if the reporters can hold their questions until the end.

And then she turns the floor over to me.

"Thank you all for coming out today. Not like you have much else to do as you're stuck in North Carolina for some football game." I smile at my sarcasm, and a light round of laughter moves through the room.

My heart is pounding as I clear my throat, my lips suddenly dry. This had been my whole life, the thing I lived, breathed and killed myself for, for a long time.

I took the leap, stepped over the edge, and started to speak.

"As most of you know, I hurt my knee last year and was traded from the team I'd thus far played my entire career with. I got to come back to the city I played for in college, and it has been an incredible season with an incredible group of team-mates and staff here at the Cheetah's organization. But as any aging athlete knows, as the years go by, your body and your stamina are not what they once were. My mind is sharper than ever, is filled with plays and ways to win, but my muscles and limbs just can't keep up. And neither can my heart, if I'm being honest. For eight years, I've poured everything into this game. I have no regrets about that. But ... it has kept me from settling down. From meeting someone special, from starting a family and a legacy. And that is something I'm looking forward to. Because after this game, after the Super Bowl, I will be retiring."

A buzz goes through the crowd, and I can hear the questions bubbling out of their throats. I look to Demi again, and she nods, and I see my future right there in her beautiful brown eyes.

I put a hand up to quiet them again. "Before you ask, this has absolutely nothing to do with anyone but myself. My teams, both of them, have always treated me with the utmost respect and professionalism. The men I've worked with, who have put their bodies on the line for me just like I have for them, have always been nothing but driven and focused. I count myself lucky to have played this many years in this league. The only thing you can attribute this retirement to is me becoming an old man."

Another round of quiet laughter.

"I wanted this to be my swan song, a Super Bowl ending if you will. And win or lose, I'm walking away with my head held high. So please, I'll take your questions, but no negativity. This is bittersweet for me, but it's more sweet than bitter. I'd like to think that my parents are looking down on me, proud of what I've accomplished and anxious to see what I'll do next."

I have to stop, to bite my fist, because I know the words I speak are true. I rarely talk about my parents to the press, but they should be involved in this moment. They sacrificed so much for me when I was growing up so that I could live this dream.

"I'd like to thank them, my mom and dad, for always believing in me, even when I didn't believe in myself. For teaching my brother and I that we could do anything we set our minds to. I'd like to thank my brother for celebrating holidays on the day after everyone else's for the past five years, because my work kept me on the road. Dylan, this year we can celebrate Christmas on December twenty-fifth just like everyone else."

The reporters laugh again.

"And last, but certainly not least, I want to thank my girl-friend. Demi," I turn to where she's standing, and I see some of the cameras focus on her, "I could have never gotten through this transitional time without you. You are the best thing that has ever happened to me, and I know that is a common phrase used, but you are. I love you, thank you for putting up with my ego and insane work schedule."

She tilted her head at me, blowing a kiss in a rare display of affection. I knew that even though she was a public figure in Charlotte, she hated the attention. But I had to acknowledge how big of a part in my life she played.

"Now, who has questions?"

They came at me full force, and for once, I was sad that soon, this wouldn't be a part of my normal Sunday.

These media days were a complete circus.

I thought I'd been around a lot of press for some of my Wish kid's outings or activities, but this was insanity. The building was the size of a gigantic airplane hangar, and backdrops for every major news or sports news organization was set up in rows. Thousands of people—fans, athletes, reporters, agents, etc.—combed the place, trying to be a part of the action.

The buzz that surrounded the day was magical, filled with excitement and nerves. It was overwhelming just standing on the sidelines, I didn't know how Pax was keeping it together.

It was the first time, and probably the last time I'd experience it due to his retirement, that I realized just how major he was to this game.

And in a way, I was extremely sad I'd missed that. That I'd been too scared, too weak, and he'd been immature and egotistical. We'd both gotten in our own ways. But at least we were together now.

Pax's hand was laced through mine as we walked from media tent to media tent, him sitting down and giving generic answers to the same questions every reporter asked.

"So, give me the inside scoop, Shaw. What do you really think of the other team?" I nudge him, winking.

It's the same question a bunch of reporters have already asked, and he's given the respectable, toe-the-line answer.

Pax leans in, kissing my hair and whispering. "Off the record? I think they're a bunch of overpaid assholes that I want to pummel into the turf. But don't tell anyone I said that."

I giggle. "My lips are sealed. Hey, where do you think you want to go to dinner after this?"

We hadn't spent a lot of time together this week, what with his busy training schedule and the interview days. I understood, but I missed him.

"I say we go up to the hotel room the team reserved for me, order a bunch of room service, and give you approximately three orgasms before it gets there."

Even though no one around us could hear any word of our conversation, I blushed. "Only if we can get mozzarella sticks."

"Shaw! Man, I thought I'd see you here. You look old, dude!"

A familiar voice has us turning around, and when I see who it's connected to, my heart jumps into my throat.

Jamison, the former outside linebacker for our college team, stands in the middle of the media frenzy, his big body taking up too much room in the wide aisle.

"Jami, good to see you! At least I don't look like you. How are those knees?" Pax was poking fun at his weight, which I never quite understand how he could move it around the field.

Jamison moves closer and narrows his eyes at me. "Wait a minute ... Demi?"

My stomach drops, because I see it in his eyes. That mockery, the secondhand embarrassment he is getting for me because I'm here with Paxton. Humiliation runs hot through me, making nausea rise in the back of my throat.

"Hi there." I give a small wave, not sure what to do. "I'm uh, going to get a cup of coffee. Over there."

I don't want to stand with them, don't want to talk to them. I feel like I'm transported right back to the days where I was an ornament instead of a respected woman.

Jamison is still talking to Pax about the game as I fill the paper cup at one of the media stands nearby.

"Man, she is still chasing that dick, huh?"

His words pull me right out of the lull that I'd been dazing in. What had he just said? Jamison was standing closer to Pax, and he thought I couldn't hear. But my cheeks burned with shame, and I stayed silent to see what would happen.

"What did you just say?" Pax's jaw clicks, and he eyes me from where I stand a few feet away.

I can feel him trying to contain his anger, exercising caution just in case we both just heard Jamison wrong.

"Demi Rosen, man. Shit, back in college, she would sink to her knees with a snap of your fingers. I guess some things never change. Desperate ho, am I right?"

My insides shut down, and tears choke me. Rage, despair, and regret consume me, and I wanted to sink into the earth and be swallowed whole. I'd gone a long time avoiding, or just altogether not remembering, people out in the world who had been witness to what Pax had put me through back then.

"You better shut your fucking mouth right now," Pax growls, stepping into Jamison like he's about to swing.

"Babe ..." I rush back over, stepping between them and pushing my boyfriend back.

I'm not even thinking about the trash Jamison just tossed all over my name, the only thing I care about is preventing the man I love from getting suspended from the last game he'll ever play. Once again, I care more about his well-being than my own.

"I'll knock your teeth so far down your throat, motherfucker.

You apologize to her, *right now.*" Pax is straining against the hands I have to his chest.

Jamison backs away, holding his hands up. "I didn't realize it was ... official now, man. I apologize. I'm happy for y'all. If banging leads to this, then sign me up for a fine-ass hookup. Matter fact, if he's still treating you like he always did, maybe you want to go out with me tonight."

He's laughing at me, basically spitting in my face. "I'm going to go."

I begin to walk away, because the shame I feel in this moment is so horrendous that I almost can't live with myself.

"Demi! *Demi!*" Pax chases after me, and at least he follows me instead of beating his ex-teammates face in.

At least he's matured enough to worry about me and not his ego.

I make it outside before he catches up to me, touching my elbow as I walk ahead of him. People on the street turn to stare, because there is a bona fide football star walking down the street in the city that has become the country's most focused-on point in the last couple of days.

"Demi, please stop," Pax pleads with me, his hand hovering on the small of my back as we walk.

I try to hold in the tears as we walk, the hotel my final desti-nation. I have to get my things, get out of here, go home to Maya. A neighbor was supposed to watch her tonight, but screw it. I needed to go home, regroup. I needed to smooth out my jumbled thoughts, my twisted heart. I was fine, better than fine. I had been happy, completely blissful in my relationship. And in two seconds, a piece of shit jock that I'd known a lifetime ago had come in and annihilated it.

He stays with me, I feel his presence and need to talk right at my back the whole time. When we finally get to the hotel, I scurry across the lobby and into the elevator. Pax gets in with me, and I immediately move to the other side, too vulnerable to look at him or let him touch me.

"Demi, I'm sorry. I'm so sorry." His voice is pained.

I curl into myself, tears finally falling, my heart audibly breaking. I'm wounded, so damaged from our past. The scars that had begun to heal, had almost been whole again, from Pax loving me ... now they were raw and bleeding.

The elevator dings on each new floor felt like a stab to the organ in my chest. I couldn't contain the sobs, and one escaped my mouth, echoing between us.

"Baby ..." Pax's arms come around me.

I back against the wall. "No!"

I didn't want him to touch me. Not right now.

When the elevator opens on our floor, I race to the room, fully intending to pack my small overnight bag and get the hell out. But Pax has other ideas.

"Demi, I'm sorry. Please talk to me, baby. I love you."

His use of those three little words right now sets me off.

"He looked at me like some cheap whore. Because that's what I was! I have to go." I couldn't be here right now, I was going to say something that I regretted.

Shoving what I'd taken out of my bag earlier back into it, I tried to make for the door.

"He's a fucking asshole, and I wish I could shove his teeth down his throat. But most of all, I want to hold you. I want to erase any fears you have. I want to repeat I love you over and over until it sinks into your brain that I'm never, ever leaving you again. You're my moon and stars now; I don't breathe, I don't function without you, baby. My whole world is black if you're not in it."

A sob burst from my lips again, because it's everything I've ever wanted to hear from him, but for the very worst reason.

"Just stay. We don't have to talk. I'll go get another room. One next door to this one. Just like the night in my apartment, I won't try a thing. But I can't stand you leaving. Not like this."

Pax's full lips pleaded, his eyes staring into my soul. So, for the second time in as many months, I relented, staying in the place he put me.

37

DEMI

I love my job. Love what I'm able to do for families. Love it when that look of pure happiness lights up a child's face.

But I also hate my job. Hate that there is a reason that these children need some hope. Hate when I see their tiny bodies suffer in the hospital.

And I especially hate it, loathe it, when I get the news that one of my special kids has passed away.

I'm just out of a relaxing bath the morning after our fight, when Paxton knocks on the door. I let him in, not raring for an argument but knowing we have to talk about it. He booked his room, slept next to me, wall to wall, all night long. I'd tossed and turned, rising early to fill the bath with bubbles and didn't leave until I was pruned, my mind was cleared, and the suds were gone.

I tell him I'm going to get dressed first, and a minute later, my cell phone rings.

He picks it up, because I'm struggling to pull up my skinny jeans, and I hear his excitement as he tells me that Sherrie, Ryan's mom, is on the phone.

A split-second later, I hear his intake of breath as, I'll later find out, she relays the details into his ear.

A viral infection. Too late to catch. Compromised his immune system and left him without a chance to fight it off.

We sit on the bed for a while after he gets off the phone with her, sobs coming through the other end as she tells us about the funeral arrangements.

"I hate this world sometimes." I choke on the tears in my throat, some of them escaping my tear ducts.

I lean into Pax, all thoughts of our fight and every insecurity I'd felt yesterday completely erased. None of it mattered when you were talking about life and death. He was here, we were in love with each other, and we were both in it for the good times and the bad.

"I know, baby. I know." He rocked me like a child as I wept in his arms, my tangled, damp hair covering his shirt as my nose became a snotty mess.

It was always horrible to lose a child, to see the families suffer, but this one cut deep. Ryan had been ... a bright light in this sometimes otherwise dark world. He had been a beam of hope, a galaxy of personality that was funny, sweet and effortlessly likable. And the fact that he'd had the same cancer as Ezra ... it was a harsh blow.

"He was so good, such a good soul." I hiccupped.

"He was the absolute best. It's not fucking fair." Pax choked out the words, and for the first time in my meltdown, I looked up to see him in pain.

He'd loved Ryan, too. "He'd brought us together that day in the park. I love you, Pax."

I meant it. I'd been hurting yesterday, but none of it mattered now.

"I love you so much." Pax touched my lips to his, an affirmation that we were okay.

When we'd tasted enough, felt our way back to even ground after yesterday's events, I pulled back. "I'm going to pay for the funeral."

It wasn't a practice I usually kept, but in certain cases, I wanted to do it. It not only helped the families, whose medical expenses had usually piled up to insurmountable bills, but it was something that marginally made me feel better. I could do something to be useful, to take the burden off their backs. I did it when I could.

"Let me help, let me contribute. I want to." Pax nodded.

I wasn't going to argue, I wanted Ryan's family to have anything they needed.

Two days later, we laid a sweet little boy to rest.

The funeral was packed, people of all ages and walks of life that Ryan had touched. Half the Cheetahs team forwent the morning practice days before the Super Bowl to be there, a lot of them remembering the glorious day when Ryan ran around playing catch with them.

There wasn't a dry eye in the place when his father took to the altar, talking about his son's radiant personality or ability to see the world in a positive light even when it had dealt him a crappy hand. He asked us all to clap for Ryan, said his son would have loved being the singular celebration of so many people. When the place erupted, I had to lean into Paxton to stop from erupting into tears on the spot.

As we left the brunch for friends and family two hours later, my eyes felt like they needed to close for the next four days.

"I don't know how you do this over and over again." Pax shook his head, his eyes bloodshot too.

I took a deep breath. "That's why I do this. If I can bring

some little sliver of good to these families for the short period of time they have together, I want to do that. No matter how much it hurts, over and over again, I know I have to do it. It heals the cracks in my heart, if only momentarily, that formed when Ezra died. I see him in every single child, and if I can give them a minute's relief from this, I'm happy to suffer the consequences afterward."

He nodded, The Eagles singing softly on the radio. "I'm so proud to know you, Demi. You are the epitome of good in this world."

Reaching my hand across the console, I laced our fingers. "Thank you for coming with me today. I've done a lot of these on mine own. It helps to have someone you love there."

"I don't know how you live after that." Pax shakes his head, the clutches of the funeral still in him.

I knew how he felt, how he couldn't let the idea of death and a small innocent child go. It felt wrong, backward. There was no way to make sense of it.

The sun had almost gone down, the day feeling impossibly long and yet it was only seven o'clock. Darkness enveloped the car, and the mild cold of early February in Charlotte seeped into my bones.

"Those parents ... how do you go on?" he chokes out, and I know he's spiraling.

I sigh, squeezing his thigh. "You just do. You're not a whole person anymore, you and I know the feeling of losing someone. But each day, each year, it gets a little more manageable. It's never easy, there are moments where you feel paralyzed with the loss, but you survive. And you remember the good moments. Cling to them, feel the pure happiness that happened during those times."

"When we have kids, I will never be able to let them out of my sight."

Paxton's words make me stop breathing, because, of course, I've thought about kids, but he just bluntly put it out there. "You want children?"

"A dozen of them, enough to man a basketball team or start our own singing group like that movie in Austria."

I laugh. "*The Sound of Music*? Okay. When are we getting started on this troupe?"

The insanity of his statement, and the giddiness I felt when talking about hypothetically starting a family with Pax overtook me. It eased the tension left behind from the funeral, and I wanted to use it to pull him out of his grief.

"I'd have started yesterday if you'd let me. Who knows, maybe my guys will just swim extra hard with some coaching."

I snort and roll my eyes. "Yeah, because that's how babies are made. You know I'm on the pill."

"So let's pull the goalie." Pax looks at me, no smile on his face.

I smack his arm. "Get out of here."

"I'm serious. Let's have a baby. It's only a matter of time before we'll want to try anyway." Now his face was beaming with excitement, and I knew he was cycling through emotions because of the trauma of today.

Palming his cheek as he swung onto the street where my condo was, I smiled. "Let's talk about it after we get through the biggest game of your career. Oh, and retirement. I think you have enough on your plate right now."

We tabled the discussion, but that night as I laid down next to him, all I could think about was a chubby little baby with Pax's eyes and my hair.

38

PAXTON

I knew from the moment I took that phone call about Ryan, that I needed to ask Demi to marry me as soon as possible.

It was kind of morbid, if you thought about it, how death reminded us about the most important things in life. It had happened when I'd lost my parents, I'd stopped fucking around both figuratively and literally, and wised up. And now, with the loss of our little friend, it made me realize that I shouldn't waste any more time where it concerned making the woman I loved my wife.

So, I'd had the ring polished, put in a new velvet lined box, and made the one call I knew was essential before I could get down on one knee.

If there isn't a puddle of sweat underneath my loafers, then my deodorant is doing its job tenfold.

I wipe my hands on my pants again, checking my watch and taking another sip of water. The waiter had asked if I wanted something stronger, but I need my head clear. Aaron Rosen already scared the shit out of me, I didn't need him running circles around me conversation wise after I'd gotten a drink in me.

He had to have some idea why I had asked him to lunch, which was probably why the son of a bitch was running late. This was an intimidation tactic, and it was working.

"Paxton." Aaron's voice, friendly but commanding, sounded from behind me.

I stood to greet him, extending my hand. "Mr. Rosen, nice to see you. Thank you for agreeing to meet me."

He shook it. "You can call me Aaron. I have a feeling we're about to become much closer anyway."

The waiter came over when he saw us sit down, and took our orders. I'd ordered a bland, high protein and vegetable dish, with little carbs. With the Super Bowl just two days away, I needed to keep to a strict diet.

After we'd settled in with drinks, I cut straight to the point.

"I think you know why I asked you here today." I paused, waiting for him to guess.

But Aaron just sat, stone-faced, waiting for me to presumably plead my case. My shirt clung to my skin, sweat rolling down my back.

"Ever since I moved back to Charlotte and saw your daughter for the first time in years, I'd realized I'd been doing it all wrong. Life, that is. Because without her, I'd just been surviving. Running on fumes. Demi, your daughter, she is the reason I came back, even if I didn't know it. Fate, and this might sound corny, intervened. I would like to marry her, sir. I'm asking for your permission. And before you question if I'm worthy enough ... just know that I'm probably not. No one really is, not for the likes of Demi. But ... I do promise to try my very hardest to become worthy. To protect her, to put her above all else, to love her and provide for her. I promise not to interfere with her success, her independent streak. So please, I came here to ask you for her hand. Would you allow me to marry your daughter?"

Aaron eyes me down, studying me as I realize he is digesting my words.

"You're not Jewish." His expression is stone when he finally speaks.

"No, sir, I'm not. But that is your daughter's choice, and I love her very much. And I don't want to dare speak for you, but I'll go out on a limb and say that you'd rather her be endlessly happy than marry someone she wasn't fully sure about just because they held the same religious beliefs."

One eyebrow raises, and I think maybe I've captured his queen in this chess match of wits. "And what about children? If I did allow you into my family, I'd be sorely disappointed if I didn't get to share my faith with my grandchildren."

I use my hands to talk. "I understand that, but again, that would be Demi and mine's choice. Although, I am not opposed to it. I want to make her happy, that is my life's mission. And if she wants that, I wouldn't stand in the way."

The waiter comes, setting our food down in front of us, and Aaron still hasn't given me an answer. I'm getting anxious, and for the first time since I came up with my plan to propose to Demi, I have some doubts that it will actually happen.

What would I do if her father said no? I know my girl, she would want me to get his permission. She's traditional, and it would mean a lot to her to have her parent's blessing on our future marriage. I can't imagine a life without her, but what would a life without her family's approval look like?

"Okay," he speaks, cutting into his steak without looking at me.

"What?" I almost didn't hear him.

Aaron puts down his utensils and levels with me. "I said, okay. You can marry my daughter. You have my permission. But if you ever, ever hurt her, Shaw, I'll saw off your balls with a dull steak knife."

To make his point, he begins cutting into the meat again, almost hacking at it. I gulp, knowing he isn't lying. But, at the same time, I'm ecstatic, adrenaline pumping through my veins at the prospect of getting down on one knee so soon.

"Thank you, Aaron. Truly, I want to become a part of your family, and plan to make your daughter very happy."

He waves me off. "Don't suck up, son. Eat your food, you have a game to prepare for. Speaking of, I heard about this retirement. Can't say I didn't agree to your future engagement with that in mind. I think it'll make for a more stable marriage if you aren't on the road half the year."

I nod. "I agree, too."

He points the knife in my direction. "But don't get complacent, a man needs to work. What do you plan to do after you hang up that jersey?"

I swallowed down my food, still nervous in his presence even though the big ask was over. "I still have endorsement deals and contracts to fulfill, so those will keep me busy. But I know I need to find something to occupy my time. I'll figure it out, as we know, I have other interests than just football."

Aaron smiles, the first non-threatening expression he's brought to this table. "I'm glad it's you, the one she is finally ready to settle down with. I like a man who isn't afraid to step up to me. Now let me tell you about my latest read, I think you'll like it, too."

As he launched into his latest novel obsession, we settled into a friendly, amicable lunch. And in the back of my mind, I realized that I wasn't just gaining a wife, I was gaining a family.

Eight Years Ago

I *was going to go early. At least, that's what my agent had told me.*

Mom, Dad and Dylan sit next to me, our table crowded into the arena that featured other top recruits from various colleges around the country. The place is alive with energy and anxiety, it's floating through the air and you could reach out and grab some if you really wanted to try.

I can't believe it's finally here. Just a week ago, I was walking my college campus, swinging my dick around like I couldn't be touched. Like I was invincible.

And I still am, but I can't help that little fish in a big pond feeling that has overwhelmed me since the combine. Which, by the way, I set records in.

"Honey, I am so proud of you." Mom wiped a tear from her eye and squeezed my hand under the table.

"Mom, will you please stop crying?" Dylan texted on his phone, rolling his eyes at her.

"It's all for you, Mom." I smiled at her, half-serious and half to make my brother look like the bad child.

"Kiss ass," Dylan mutters.

"Holy cow, that's John Elway." Dad was like a giddy school boy.

"Pretty fucking cool, right?" I joined in on his excitement, because it was surreal seeing so many of your idols in one room.

"Paxton, language!" Mom scolded me.

I tipped my head in apology, and then pulled at my shirt collar, the tie only making me sweat more than I already was. Some brand, I forget the name, had paid me a chunk of money just to wear their suit today. How insane was that? They paid me. That's what this was going to be like, the next level in this sport. Sure, college football had brought pretty pussy and free drinks, some nice gear … but this was big time.

Being a professional football player meant advertisement deals and campaigns, the chance to design my own gear, or get into my own product line. I had no idea what that would be, but hell, I had the resources at my fingertips if I made good on my talent in the game.

"Son, I just want you to take a deep breath. If you don't go first, nothing changes. It's an honor just to be here." Dad patted my shoulder.

My parents were the best, always grounding my brother and me and showing us the fair, modest way. I'd lost some of that, being away from them at school. Part of my conscience burned every time I pulled a dick move on campus or at a bar, or with a random girl in a random room.

But now that I was here with them, something had fallen back into place. I didn't feel like answering my father with some snide remark, like I would have to one of my buddies in our fraternity house. I really wanted to listen to him, take his genuine advice and apply it. I wanted to let my mom boast about me, give me a gold star. I was like a damn preening kindergartner, and it might be a sissy thing to be, but right now I was just going to let it happen.

"Got it, Dad." I nodded at him, serious.

It had been a long time since my family had all been together. I had a bowl game over Christmas break, so I wasn't able to get home. Then Mom and Dad had flown out to me for my birthday in April, and Dylan had come to visit back in February. I know he went home for the holidays, but we hadn't all been together as a four-unit family since ... last year?

And suddenly I realized how hard it was going to be to get the four of us together when I was traveling and training every week. The league was a thousand times more demanding than college, and a pang of sadness hit me in the gut that I would be alone a majority of my life now.

The draft started, the music dramatic and kind of cheesy, but exactly what this kind of moment called for.

"Massachusetts is on the clock with the first draft pick in this first round," the master of ceremonies announced into the microphone on stage.

It only took my home team, the one I was rooting for to take me, one minute and six seconds to solidify their pick.

And when the current running back of the team, the one I'd idolized for six seasons, came to the mic, bent down, and said my name, I could hardly believe it.

The room erupted around me, Mom jumped up and hugged my neck, crying into it, her tears wetting the lapel of my suit. Dad had the proudest look on his face that I'd ever seen, and even Dylan stood to bump my fist. And then told me to get him season tickets.

But as I stood up on that stage, shaking hands and holding up a jersey with my name on the back, I couldn't help but look down at the crowd.

See the other players, squeezing their girlfriend's hands.

Some of them had wives, children.

They were more focused on them than what pick they were or

what city they'd uproot their lives to. Had people they were going to be able to come home to and share this journey with.

And for the first time in my life, I thought that maybe I'd made a mistake when it came to women. Typically, I'd one and done them. They were little more than a sexy, flirty distraction.

Except right now, I wanted to know what Demi Rosen thought about me going number one. I had this urge to lie in her bed with her, talking after we'd fucked each other's brains out. There was this yearning in me, to know if she was watching and if she was happy. Not just for me, but in life. I'd left without so much as a wave or a nod, and now I kind of felt bad about that.

Standing up on the biggest stage of my life, and I was thinking about a woman.

And now it was probably too late to do anything about that.

"I know it's not your perfect rooftop patio, but it was the best I could do on short notice."

I swing open the door, and the night air greets us. Pax follows me out.

"How did you pull this off? Do I even want to know?" Pax kissed me on the cheek, looking up.

"I may or may not have pulled the bellboy aside, gave him a fifty, and convinced him that this was what Paxton Shaw needed to guarantee this city a Super Bowl win." I shrugged.

He chuckled. "The press would have a field day if they got a hold of this."

"Eh, who cares, you're retiring tomorrow." I walk to him, leaning in and resting my head against him as I looked up.

"How did you know this would be exactly what I needed tonight?" He cradles me into his warmth.

"Because I know you, Paxton Shaw. And I wanted to sneak out with you, teenage dream style."

"Our parents might find out ... or Coach. Then I'd be in big trouble. Technically, I should be sleeping right now."

"I won't tell anyone." I put a finger to my lip, and he bites it. "I have another surprise."

Revealing my basket, I pull out a picnic blanket and some snacks. I set it up, all as he watches with a small smile gracing his lips the entire time.

Pulling a bottle of sparkling cider out, I wave my hand à la Vanna White. "Just like our picnic date that you tricked me into."

Pax booms out a laugh, sitting down next to me. "I had to do something, you were shunning all of my advances. With good reason, I have to say, but still, a guy needed a break."

I poured us some cider into the plastic champagne flutes I'd brought and handed him one. "To Ryan."

He'd brought us together, I owed that little boy so much. We clinked glasses, a bittersweet note filling the air as we drank.

"We owe it all to him." Pax spoke my thoughts for the millionth time since we'd come back together. "You think he's up there?"

He pointed to the stars above us, a tapestry of light illuminating the rooftop.

"I know he is. Probably giggling down at us when we kiss and shouting out plays that you need to complete tomorrow. He'll be sitting right on that fifty-yard line, I believe it."

"That's for sure. He knew his football." Pax ate some of the spread I'd brought for us, never not hungry.

"Are you nervous for tomorrow?" I never really asked him about games, because generally I didn't know all that much.

He shook his head. "Not really. I always think of the Super Bowl as the one game where I get to have fun."

I study him, confused. "Fun? Isn't it like, the most pressure you ever have on you?"

Pax's hand finds mine, almost like it was an unconscious movement. "Exactly the opposite actually. There is nothing on the line, not really. Sure, the glory of winning, of hoisting that trophy ... but, there is nothing after that. This game isn't one we have to win, at all costs. We aren't trying to preserve a record or make it into the playoffs. This is just for bragging rights, for victory. It's the one time that we, at least I think this way, can play for that little boy who fell in love with the game."

It was poetic, in a way, and I understood it. "So, go out there tomorrow and have fun."

He smiled. "Exactly. Especially as my last game I'll ever put pads on for. It seems surreal. I've done this for so long. What will I do now?"

I scooted over to him, lying with my back to his front, as we tilted up to look at the stars. "Be a stay at home dad?"

I could feel Pax's entire body go rigid. "Is there something you need to tell me?"

Just to tease him, I waited a beat, and then burst into laughter. "No, there isn't. But maybe someday soon there could be."

He settled down again, playing with my hair in his fingers. "I'd like that a lot. Yeah, stay at home dad. You go out and be the bread winner, Mrs. CEO."

"And that doesn't bother you?" I needed to know if my running a business was something he would be comfortable with in the long run.

A lot of men said that they didn't mind, that they liked a strong woman. But when it really came down to it, I'd heard of and seen many situations where the relationship fell apart because a man couldn't handle a woman's success. I know Pax had been supportive and understanding of my demanding schedule thus far, but getting more serious—marriage, raising a family, having a future—that would just mean more time away from him.

"Of course, it doesn't. I mean that, I think it's so important the work that you do. And that you're a boss, in the slang and traditional sense. You inspire me to work harder, what I've done is nothing compared to what you've built. I'm secure enough to be completely okay with your success."

I smiled, nuzzling into him. "Good. Now be quiet, I'm trying to stargaze."

Pax chuckled, but didn't say anything further.

We stayed out on the roof for another hour, longer than we probably should have. But it was a nice night, and the relaxing feeling of being together, in the quiet, after a week of chaos, was too good to pass up. It felt like we were on the precipice of some-thing enormous. This big game, Paxton's retirement.

But something else, too.

And I couldn't place my finger on it, but after tomorrow, it felt like the entire world was going to change.

PAXTON

My teammates flank me, our hands over our hearts as a country singer I didn't recognize belted out a beautiful rendition of the National Anthem.

I lock eyes with Connor, who nods, black streaks of tar paint smeared under his eyes. My gaze scours the stadium, taking in the scents and sounds that have become my theme song, my soundtrack, for the past eight years.

This is it. The last game. I knew for a while that it was coming, but I wasn't fully prepared for the emotion clutching my heart and bringing unshed tears to the back of my throat.

I found them in the stands, in the family suite that sat just above the fifty-yard line, at the top of the first section of seats. Demi stood with her hand over her heart, my jersey underneath her big parka jacket. She looked breathtaking, my lucky charm, my second chance. How fucking lucky was I that she had given me one? That was divine intervention if I ever saw it. A gift from the stars.

On one side of her stood Dylan, his face painted with my number drawn out in white paint. He looked like a total groupie, and I had to laugh at his enthusiasm.

And on the other side was Sarah and Aaron. They'd been so thrilled when I'd sent them tickets, told them I wouldn't want them to miss this big moment. Little did they know that the moment they weren't supposed to miss wasn't the actual game, but the grand gesture after it was over.

The anthem ended, and our team moved into a huddle, Coach delivering one of the most motivating pump up speeches I'd ever heard.

"Men, we've worked damn hard this season. Overcome all of the odds stacked against us. No one thought we would be here in the end. But here we fucking are! Go out there and play the best four quarters of your life. Leave nothing unanswered, nothing stays out on that field! Sixty minutes of glory, that's what I want from you. Hands in!"

We all put them in, the circle of brawn and courage buzzing with raw energy that could spark an explosion.

As soon as the first whistle blows, our special team's unit receives the punt and the receiver runs the ball out to the forty. Time to go to work, and I can feel the blood coursing through my veins. I can practically hear it, flowing overtime and giving me this adrenaline high that is indescribable.

I line up, the cornerback covering me giving me some sneer and trash talk that I don't even bother to listen to. This is my game, he has no business even being on my field. Some of the youth and cockiness floods over me, and I'm transported back to the hotshot know-it-all who used to make risky plays that some-times paid off, and sometimes didn't. That ego combined with my knowledge now is what will get me through this.

Play after play, we advance, scoring or picking up first downs. It feels like time is standing still, and for the first time in a year, I don't feel the aches and pains of old age as an athlete plaguing my body. It's like the universe is allowing me to give the game of football one last shot, scratch free. My knee is mobile, the tendons flex and muscles tense, without having to favor the other leg or go easy on it.

I put every ounce of myself into the last drives, trying to see the game through the eyes of the little boy who fell in love with it.

Because it will be his last time, my last time, under the lights.

Ticker tape is everywhere.

In my hair, in my mouth, fluttering down from the sky like stars that have exploded into our team colors.

It's a sea of people, cameras, new championship merchandise being flung at me or pulled over my head. My teammates are crying, happy tears, and reporters are shoving microphones in my face, trying to get a quote from the one guy who is on top of the world right now.

It was my swan song. The last game. A ring. Going out as a champion.

My body, my heart, my mind, they all sing with triumph. And there is only one person I want to share it all with right now.

I see her through the crowd, her milk chocolate-colored hair waving wildly as she congratulates person after person, every other second jumping up and down next to Dylan in disbelief.

Moving people out of the way, dodging cameras and handshakes, I finally make my way to her.

"Baby!" she screams, hugging my neck and all but jumping into my arms.

I bury my nose in her hair, squeezing her tight to me, basking in this moment. She's the only one I want by my side for every moment in life. It took me a long time coming to realize that.

Placing her down, I sink to one knee, pulling the ring box from my football pants. I'd had the thing in my extra helmet on the sidelines all game. I held it up to her.

"Demi Rosen, I'm done with this chapter. Now, I want to start my next one. The one where we live happily ever after. Now, I know you deal in wishes, so I'd like you to grant mine. Marry me. Make me the luckiest man on the face of this earth. The luckiest man in the galaxy."

People around us start to catch on, there are some shrieks and wolf whistles. Then the crowd begins to cheer, they must have this playing on the Jumbotron.

But I'm only focused on Demi, her expression priceless. She stands stock-still, her mouth hanging open, tears glistening in her beautiful brown eyes. I wait her out, trying not to ask again because I know she's in shock.

"Answer the boy, *bubbala!*" Her mom nudges her, both of her parents looking on in surprised awe.

I look at her, really look at her, inching the ring toward her.

"Yes," she whispers, her eyes boring into me, tears spilling down her cheeks.

I don't wait on my knee any longer, which is starting to throb, and instead jump up to lift her in celebration. She squeals and buries her head in my shoulder.

"I love you so much," I whisper into her hair.

"I love you. I've loved you for a long time," she whispers back.

Someone around us yells, "She said yes!"

Flashbulbs come from every direction, and people rush us, pulling Demi away from me. I laugh, the whole atmosphere just one of huge celebration. I make my way to her again.

"I think I need to give you something to seal the deal." I take her left hand, putting the ring on her third finger.

Studying it on her hand, Demi puts her other one to her mouth. "It's so beautiful. Pax, I can't believe this."

I gaze at it on her hand, knowing that it is exactly where it belongs. That ring is home. "It was my mother's."

A gasp, and then tears. "This is the most special ring you ever could have picked. I promise I will cherish it forever."

Taking her face in my hands, I kiss her lightly and then lean my forehead in to hers. "I know you will, because I'll never let you take it off. You're mine. Forever."

And then chaos takes over again. Her parents smother her, as Dylan shakes me by the shoulders and shouts about being the best man and sitting on a float in the Super Bowl parade. The press surrounds us, asking questions about my game and the engagement.

Through it all though, I'm looking at Demi. My future wife.

One Month Later

"Please tell me again why we are doing this?"

I suck in, the air in my lungs burning as I hear the zipper on the back of the dress zip up.

"Chelsea, if you don't want to be supportive, you don't have to be here," I half-joke.

The seamstress taps me on the shoulder, signaling that I can turn around and walk out.

I'm halfway out of the fitting room when my best friend answers again. "I don't mean this, as in trying on wedding dresses. I mean, why are we doing this so soon? Don't people wait a little before starting to plan a wedding? Much less actually have one in less than ninety days."

The delicate layers of tulle waft around me as I look at the panel of people before me. "Mom, are you going to cry at every single one?"

She blows her nose, sobbing again. "You just look so beautiful!"

Leave it to my mother to be even more of a bridezilla than

any of the brides in this bridal dress salon. She sits next to Farrah, who looks like she might be allergic to my mother's crying. Chelsea sits next to my coworker, and Hillary, who I have become close with even as Paxton goes through retirement, looks on as well. They've all assembled to make my bridal party, and have been a huge help scrambling to make our wedding happen.

After the initial shock and celebration of the Super Bowl and our engagement wore off, which took about a week, my fiancé announced he would like to get married as soon as possible. As in, tomorrow, and he wasn't kidding. I put him off a little, saying that I'd been dreaming about this moment and that if we didn't give my mother a fairy-tale wedding, she'd Jewish guilt us both to death.

So here I was, trying to find my dream wedding dress in a week, so that we could get married in two months. I'd already hired the photographer, a friend of Hillary's who did their family portraits here in Charlotte. We'd booked a venue, which was surprisingly easy with my event planning contacts. I was using the same florist I did for every annual Wish Upon a Star gala, and Paxton was in charge of the band and hotel accommodations. It might be a whirlwind, but I was surprised at how easily everything was coming together.

"And, Chels, they usually do. But we've wasted so much time, you know that more than anyone." I raised a brow at her. "So, tell me if you like this one?"

I waved a hand to model it for them. The dress had a full, fluffy skirt with tiny crystal flowers all over it. The straps were illusion and wide with a deep V to my cleavage, but still modest. It was gorgeous, and a little flutter went through my stomach as I waited for them to respond.

"Well, I don't dislike it as much as that mermaid crap you were talking about before, so I'm sold!" Farrah smiled.

She was my rational thinker during this time, keeping me on track and on budget.

"I think this is the one!" Hillary clapped, always positive. She and Mom were on the same page, and my mom smiled and nodded through hysterics.

"I love it. You look incredible. But then again, you look incredible in anything. Oh, and if Paxton Shaw ever hurts you, I told him I'd cut his ding-a-ling off and shove it down his throat." Chelsea made the slice-across-her-throat motion.

Okay, so she was still a little skeptical of my husband-to-be, but she was coming around.

Farrah laughed hysterically. It seemed that my college best friend and my work best friend were a match made in heaven. They'd already set up a happy hour for all of us tomorrow night and were calling it the bachelorette before the bachelorette. I'm pretty sure they were forcing me to have the ever-popular girls trip simply so they could party their asses off, but I was happy to do it for them.

"I really think this is the one, Demi," Hillary spoke again, nodding like an experienced stylist. She was my fellow fashion lover; we prayed at the altar of shoes and purses. "Can we see that veil? No, not the fingertip one, the cathedral. Every woman deserves to wear a cathedral veil once in her life. I plan on wearing one at least three times."

"Does that mean you'll have three husbands?" Chelsea asked.

Hillary waved her hand. "Oh lord no, one husband is all I can handle. No, I'll make Charles marry me two more times. For the romance of it, but mostly so I can buy two more wedding dresses that are completely different than the one I wore the first time."

My mom started to laugh. "Isn't that the truth? One husband is surely enough. That's why they want you to get it right the first time, because trying to find another one is completely exhausting. Not to mention, I will never wash another man's underwear. No, thank you."

Chels hugged my mom as she laughed. "Amen to that, Mama Rosen!"

The consultant put the veil on me, clipping it into my hair, and bringing me earrings to go with it.

"Oh no, she won't be wearing those." My mom shooed her away, and I smiled at her.

I knew why she didn't want me to put them in. "You still want me to wear them?"

Mom nodded, tears wetting both of our eyes. "Of course, I do, your grandmother would want you to wear her pearls."

Before she'd passed, my grandma would tell me all the time how she couldn't wait to see her pearl and diamond studs, her most prized possession, on the lobes of her only granddaughter on her wedding day. And now I was going to do just that.

When everything else was fastened and zipped, I turned, looking in the three-panel mirror at the end of the little runway the salon had in the middle of the store.

And my mouth dropped. I looked like a bride. A full-fledged, fairy-tale, white Christmas ornament, bride. "Oh my God ..."

"That's the reaction we were looking for. Sold, we'll take it!" Chels whirled her hand around, signaling to the bridal consultant to pack it up. "Now, let's go have a drink. I've fulfilled my maid of honor duties and need a stiff martini."

With tears in my eyes, I laughed. "Okay fine, let's go pay you in blue cheese stuffed olives. But, I don't think I'm going to take this off until the wedding day. So, I can wear this for another two months, right?"

43

When Chelsea had proposed a joint bachelor/bachelorette party, I had been skeptical.

I wanted Demi to have her space with her girl-friends. And selfishly ... I wanted to have my last night of free-dom, doing stupid shit with my guys friends.

But two months after the Super Bowl, and here we were. Four shots and two beers down, everyone was drunk, giddy, and ready for a weekend of all out partying and fun.

"Dance with me!" Demi hung around my neck, her skimpy white dress silky against my fingertips.

She looked like sex on legs, very long legs with impossibly high heels at the bottom. The dress sank low in the front and back, so much so that I could feel her skin every time I brushed against her on the dance floor. And enough to drive me crazy with jealousy anytime another set of eyes fell across her.

"Anything for you, my bride," I shouted, the music thumping in the air.

We had gone to Ocean City, Maryland, the world's capital for bachelor and bachelorette weekends. We'd already day drank in the ocean, gone to a long dinner with lots of laughs and drinking, and now we were just basically drinking and dancing. Again. It was exactly how this weekend should go.

"Ew, that sounds morbid! I don't like 'my bride.'" Drunk Demi was bubbly and talkative, a little bit less reserved than her normal self.

It reminded me of college ... the good times at least. The flirty anticipation we'd had each night, how attracted to her I was. Now it was a thousand times better, because I'd put my asshole stupidity behind me and recognized how amazing it was that I got to go home and stay home with her each night.

"Okay, what do you like?" My head swam with drink, but my limbs sung with happiness and horniness.

She sloshed her cranberry and vodka, the purple and blue lights of the club dancing across her face. "I like baby, babe, sweetie, bunny, gorgeous, sexy, and Mrs. Shaw."

My cock jumped when she said her future last name. "Mrs. Shaw, huh? I'll call you that all night, baby."

"Stop flirting with your fiancé! This is supposed to be your last romp of freedom! Let your boobies out!" Chelsea ran up, breaking us apart and squeezing Demi's boobs.

"You're the one who made this a joint party!" Demi giggled.

Anthony came over, swaying, and I knew he hadn't drank this much in years. "I love my wife, I love being a dad. Did you guys know we are having a baby boy?"

He'd only told anyone in the club who would listen, and then he told them again. But he was excited, and I was happy for the guy.

"Get this man a shot!" Connor came over, a blinking necklace of beads around his neck.

"Hey, where did you get those?" Farrah grabbed at them.

Connor swung away, but I could see his eyes lingering on her cleavage. "Show me your bra and maybe I'll give them up."

We were a merry band of idiots, and I couldn't think of a better bunch to get rip roaring drunk and sloppy with.

"We're in Maryland, not New Orleans. Nice try, buddy." Farrah grinned madly at him, like she'd just made the point of the century.

"Oh my God, let's go to New Orleans! I want a beignet!" Demi suddenly screams. "Quick, you can get a private plane or something, right baby?"

She's looking at me like I can pull one out of thin air. "Slow down, Speed Racer. We're staying right here. And what do you think I am, a millionaire?"

"Aren't you?" Chelsea points at me, slurring.

"Point taken. Are you just marrying me for my money, Demi Rosen?"

This makes my woman giggle. "I think you're marrying me for mine. Gold digger!"

Connor runs over to the stage, yelling up at the DJ. All of a sudden, Kanye West's famous hit comes on, and all of the girls throw their hands in the air, letting out whooping shouts. I take Demi's hips, smashing her back to my front, rubbing my growing cock on the backside that I love and admire.

"You got a boyfriend?" I tease her.

"Actually, I'm getting married." She wiggles her ring finger at me. "But I'm single for the weekend. Bachelorette trip."

I raise my eyebrows, molding us together as the beat invades our veins. "How funny! I'm here for my bachelor party."

"Hmm, well, I envy the girl who gets to marry you." She grins.

"Hey, how about we spend our last trip of freedom together? I saw a quiet place we can ... talk." I'm playing along.

Demi exaggerates a frown. "I won't cheat on my fiancé."

I coax her, brushing her hair to the side and kissing her neck. "What happens in Ocean City stays in Ocean City."

She melts, goose bumps moving across all of that exposed skin, as I explore her collarbone with my lips. We don't agree on it, but the next minute I'm pulling her along, heading for the small alcove I'd seen on the way in. It was tucked in the corridor where the bathrooms were located, a dark hallway with purple velvet walls that was muted from the sounds of the club, nothing but the thump of the beat invading here.

Demi followed me, her breathing quick and excited, as I led us down the hall, and into the cutout in the wall. Who knew what this space was supposed to be used for ... possibly phone calls or a smoke break if it was too cold? I didn't care, because right now, I was going to fuck my sexy ass fiancée in here.

"Take off your underwear," I growled, unbuckling my belt.

My cock was screaming at me at this point, so hard and pounding with blood that I needed release.

"I'm not wearing any," Demi pants.

That has me grabbing her, pushing her up against the wall so that her hands rest at her shoulders, and her cheek touches the velvety surface. Hiking up her dress, I thrust my fingers into her pussy, finding it wet and waiting for me.

"Fucking hell, babe." I have to steady myself, because the aroma of her and the liquor in my system has me stumbling.

"Oh, Pax ..." she moans, loudly, and I have to slap my other hand over her mouth.

"Shh, quiet, baby. Someone will catch us." I can barely breathe I'm so turned on.

"Let them, I don't care." Demi is writhing between me and the wall.

Fuck. I have to be in her now. She's about to combust and I want to feel it.

Removing myself roughly from my pants, I grab one of her hips, and line myself up with the other hand. I push on her back, and she bends to my will.

"Hold on, baby."

I see her hand tense on the wall, and then I drive in until my balls slap against her clit.

"Oh my God!" she practically screams, and if anyone is in the bathroom, they can definitely hear this.

Hell, people in the club can probably hear this.

I don't care at this point, nothing else but my cock buried insider her wetness registering. My hips slam against her ass, over and over as I wrench her hips back against me. She's got her hand in her mouth, biting down on it while trying not to scream.

"I love you, Mrs. Shaw. Come for me, Mrs. Shaw," I growl at her.

And as if she was doing it on command, I feel her walls tighten around me, a careening cry bursting from Demi's lips.

I follow just on the heels of her orgasm, my climax ripping through me as I shoot my cum into her. I can barely breath as I lean against the wall. I stroke her hip, loving the feel of her sweat on my fingers.

The haze of lust lifts off slowly, but when clearer heads prevail, Demi starts to chuckle.

She turns her head, kissing my cheek. "I think we better get back to our bridal party before they realize we've gone off to have sex."

J ames Taylor plays in the background, singing about going to Carolina, and I'm with him. There is no place I'd rather be.

The curtains in our, yes, *our*, condo are drawn to the outside world. I lie on the couch, flipping like a gerbil through the channels, trying to find a movie we'll both like. Thrillers for Demi, inspirational sports movies for me ... go figure.

My fiancée hums in the kitchen, the dog futzing around at her feet. I admire her, watching her sway her hips in those sweatpants that somehow make her ass look more enticing than when she is naked. It's a mystery how she does that ... keeps me coming back for more just when I think I know every part of her intimately.

She brings over the tray, complete with Twizzlers, coffee ice cream, and a chocolate porter beer.

"Marry me, my dream girl." I smirk, catching her by the waist and pulling her down on top of me.

She giggles, a dark curtain of hair cocooning us both. "Can't. My father would put you through the bris you never had if you didn't get his permission."

Demi is joking, the ring on her finger gleaming in the TV light. "Hell, I'd walk through fire for you. But I don't think I'd cut my dick off, sorry, babe. That's where I draw the line."

"I guess we'll just have to run away. Again." My mind wanders back to our incredible vacation that we returned from just days ago, to celebrate my retirement.

Not that I was actually retired. Two days after getting back from the much-needed vacation to Aruba that Demi and I took to unwind, Anthony came to me and offered me a job. I was going to be working part time at his training facility, helping to strengthen and rehabilitate the same athletes I just won a championship with.

Obviously, I didn't need the money, but I loved the game of football, and I could never fully walk away. I also needed to get out of the house, as Demi said. After I'd sent her my thousand pictures of Maya and me cuddling on the couch, she told me I needed to get a hobby. And I'd agreed.

"I can't wait to marry you." I hold her on top of me, doing a crunch of sorts to connect our lips.

Demi submits to me, our tongues tangling, dancing and slowly stoking the flames of arousal.

Suddenly, she sits up, a look that I can't place gracing her beautiful face.

"Do you think that Jamison, or any of your friends, will say anything after they see we're getting married?" Worry lines crease her face.

I tried to wipe them away, using the back of my hand to caress her skin. "They wouldn't dare. And if they do, who cares? That is in our past. I can admit that I was a smug, cocky asshole. I'm not afraid of apologizing and owning up. It doesn't matter anyway, that's between us."

Demi nodded, feeding Maya the end of her Twizzler. "You're right. In fact, this is the last we're talking about it."

"Except for me to say one last time, that I'm truly sorry for it all. And that if I could do it all over again ... well, I guess I wouldn't. I wish I hadn't wasted so much time, but we were meant to come together in this way. What is that thing you're always saying?"

"If it's written in the stars, then it is fated to happen." She smiled, repeating her phrase.

"And my marrying you is fated to happen. I'll be the one down in front, waiting for you under the stars." I smooth a lock of hair behind her ear.

It had been my idea to get married after dark, on the rooftop of one of the most well-known hotels in Charlotte. It would overlook the city, and I had worked tirelessly with the venue to transform it into a magical garden. Demi didn't know the extent of the work I'd put in. But hey, when you were a retired old fart, you had nothing else to do.

"Tomorrow, babe." Demi smiled, a radiant expression that stretched from ear to ear.

"Isn't it bad luck to sleep with the bride the night before the wedding?"

She eyed me. "Are you complaining about having your soon-to-be wife on top of you?"

"Not in the slightest, Mrs. Shaw." Saying that sent a wave of pleasure through me.

"Gosh, do I love hearing that." Demi's eyes fluttered shut, as if she was savoring the sound of her married name.

A devilish smile played at my lips. "And I love you. Now, let's go practice consummating our marriage."

EPILOGUE

DEMI

One Year Later

Moonlight streamed through the thin curtains, the sound of summer crickets creating a nighttime chorus as I walked through the hallway on tiptoes.

I creaked open the door, careful to step over the sleeping form of a protective dog. Maya never relented her post these days, choosing to leave our bed in the middle of the night to come in here.

Wiping the sleep from my eyes, I smiled, because no matter how tired I was, this was always worth it.

It seemed like a lifetime ago that I'd wait up, anticipating a call from Pax in the middle of the night. A midnight summoning, my heart like a slave to his.

And now, I was a slave to our son, my heart completely and utterly his.

"You're caught." I hear a gruff voice from behind me and feel my husband's arms snake around my waist.

Leaning back, I press a finger to his lips. "Don't wake him."

Paxton nuzzles my hair, whispering, "I'm not the one

standing in here in the middle of the night. Especially when I should be trying to get some rest."

I sigh, wrapping my arms around his that are wrapped around me. "I know, I know. I just can't stop looking at him. He's just so beautiful."

"Ryan Ezra Shaw, you have stolen your mommy's heart away from me." Pax chuckles quietly.

"Not stolen, expanded. I never thought I'd have enough room in me to love one Shaw man, let alone two. But now I can't imagine anything else."

We stand in silence, watching our two-week-old son sleep. It's been a whirlwind, this past year. First the Super Bowl win, and then Pax's retirement, our wedding, and then finding out we would be adding to our family.

Nothing like getting pregnant on your honeymoon. The first day to be exact, as was the case with us. Paxton had gotten his wish; he'd knocked me up at the first possible second that I'd allowed him to. And now here we were, standing over our sleeping baby, completely and utterly smitten. We'd named him after two of the most important little boys in our lives; the one who had brought us together, and the one that felt like a part of me even after he was gone.

"How is it that he's only been here for two weeks, and I already forget what life was like before him?" Pax marveled.

"I know. Even Maya doesn't mind his crying at night." I smiled, gazing down at the fluffy dog below.

"Come on, we should get back to bed. Lord knows he'll be up in an hour, wanting to taste some of that milk." Pax's hands grazed my breasts, and then moved down to lace fingers with my own.

I giggled softly as we walked out of the nursery. "How many times have I told you, you're not getting any breast milk."

"Come on, just a tiny drop? I think it's so hot." His eyes heated as we made our way back into our own bedroom.

"And get that horny look out of your gorgeous eyes. The doctor said six weeks before sex. Or do you want to have another one?" I scolded him as he helped me back into bed.

I was still a lot tender and a little sore from a human working its way out of my body.

"Is that even a question? Of course, let's go right now!" Pax slid in between the sheets next to me, resting his hand on my thigh.

I had to laugh. "I love you."

It was absolutely nuts how life could change in just a moment. Like a shooting star, something could grace you with its presence and light up the entire world, changing your fate forever.

I never thought I could be happy after Pax had left all of those years ago. I'd tried, I'd hated him, I'd moped and then attempted to move on. He'd changed, he'd grown, he'd gone through something so life altering that it made him question every decision.

And then we'd been brought back together, and my heart was suddenly whole. For all of the heartbreak we had gone through, it was destined that we'd end up together. I truly believed that.

I was no longer sneaking around in the dark to be with him. We were here together. With our little star lighting up our world, shining love into corners of our hearts that we didn't even know existed.

Want to read another angsty, second chance romance? Pick up <u>*Down We'll Come, Baby*</u> today!

ALSO BY CARRIE AARONS

Do you want your **FREE** Carrie Aarons eBook?

All you have to do is **sign up for my newsletter**, and you'll immediately receive your free book!

Then, check out all of my books, available in Kindle Unlimited!

Standalones:

If Only in My Dreams

Foes & Cons

Love at First Fight

Nerdy Little Secret

That's the Way I Loved You

Fool Me Twice

Hometown Heartless

The Tenth Girl

You're the One I Don't Want

Privileged

Elite

Red Card

Down We'll Come, Baby

As Long As You Hate Me

On Thin Ice

All the Frogs in Manhattan

Save the Date

Melt

When Stars Burn Out

Ghost in His Eyes

Kissed by Reality

The Prospect Street Series:

Then You Saw Me

The Callahan Family Series:

Warning Track

Stealing Home

Check Swing

Control Artist

Tagging Up

The Rogue Academy Series:

The Second Coming

The Lion Heart

The Mighty Anchor

The Nash Brothers Series:

Fleeting

Forgiven

Flutter

Falter

The Flipped Series:

Blind Landing

Grasping Air

ABOUT THE AUTHOR

Author of romance novels such as Fool Me Twice and Love at First Fight, Carrie Aarons writes books that are just as swoonworthy as they are sarcastic. A former journalist, she prefers the love stories of her imagination, and the athleisure dress code, much better.

When she isn't writing, Carrie is busy binging reality TV, having a love/hate relationship with cardio, and trying not to burn dinner. She lives in the suburbs of New Jersey with her husband, two children and ninety-pound rescue pup.

Please join her readers group, Carrie's Charmers, to get the latest on new books, exclusive excerpts and fun giveaways.

You can also find Carrie at these places:

Website
Amazon
Facebook
Instagram
TikTok
Goodreads

Printed in Great Britain
by Amazon